NIGHT HUNTER

N GRAY

VINCI

BOOKS

By N Gray

Shifter Days, Vampire Nights & Demons in Between

Twisted

Lady Hawk and Her Mountain Man

Hidden Shifter

Wolf

Wolf Retreat

Night Hunter

The Fixer

Kai

Lee

Flynn

Jude

Scout Thorne

The Secret Tomb

Murder of Crows

Blaire Thorne

Ulysses Exposed

Voodoo Priest

Butterflies and Hurricanes

Salvation

Underworld Legacy

The Dana Mulder Suspense Thriller Series

Deadly Pattern

Devil Mountain

Chasing Evil

Nightcrawler

Horror

What's for Dinner

Creature Features

Monster Features

Thrillers

Lady Killer

More from N Gray

writing as Natalie Michaels

Steve Campbell Psychological Suspense Thrillers

The Last Girl

The Bone Forest

The White Dahlia

I See You

Death in the City

More from N Gray

writing as SD Syns

The Diaries

Red Lace Diaries

www.ngraybooks.com

Vinci Books

vinci-books.com

Published by Vinci Books Ltd in 2026

1

Chapter One

DECLAN

Watson shuffled into the room, interrupting my meal. I narrowed my eyes at his feet, hoping they'd get chopped off. His shuffling was annoying. Luckily, he only did it on airplanes; it had something to do with balance. I couldn't remember, I wasn't listening when he told me.

I let go of my meal and offered Watson my attention when he cleared his throat at the foot of my bed.

"What is it, Watson?"

He growled, furrowing his brows. "Winston."

"What?"

"My name is Winston, Master. After all these centuries, surely your memory hasn't started to fade."

I arched an eyebrow at the jab and Watson bowed low; almost over doing it.

"Forgive me, Master."

"All right. Now what do you want… Winston." I drawled.

"The pilot will start our descent in about an hour."

1

"Good, will you clean up this mess?" I pushed the corpse away from my body and climbed out of bed.

"Yes, Master."

"It's a pity though, she was such a good lay, even showed me a trick or two," I grinned, wiggling my eyebrows.

Winston averted his eyes. He wasn't a prude and had seen me naked too many times to count, yet he never stared at me when I stood in all my splendor.

"Why did you kill her then?"

"I couldn't help myself." I was sure the Council would have a fit, but at this moment I didn't care. "And besides, with my tasting limited, I simply couldn't stop. I desperately needed a full meal. The moment her blood touched the inside of my mouth." I licked my lips and tasted a drop of blood I'd missed. "I couldn't stop until her heart did. I'll be full for at least a day." My smile reached my eyes.

"Very well, Master."

"Thank you, Watson." I sauntered to the bathroom to freshen up for our descent and ignored Winston's sigh and the rolling of his eyes.

Winston was such a good sport. I'd been teasing him for years. Who named their child Winston, anyway? How dreadfully awful. And this was centuries ago. Never mind, he was a wonderful man servant and would never leave me.

I stared at my physique in the mirror; a mirror made without silver. Unfortunately, some still weren't able to see themselves. But I was old and powerful enough to see my reflection, toned body and sculptured cheeks. My blue eyes twinkled even. That girl's blood did wonders for my skin. I should stick to under twenties. But never younger than eighteen—a pervert I was not.

My fangs retracted, leaving me with blunt teeth once more. I dared not scare the riff-raff at the airport. I chuckled to myself, imagining the chaos I'd cause. Vampires had been living out in the open for years, but humans still feared us. As they should.

I showered, washed my hair and dried my body. Once back in my room, I chose a simple outfit, black pants, black T-shirt, my black coat and boots. I was still in my gothic phase and doubted I'd ever leave it. Black, ever elegant, was my color of choice. Red was my second color, naturally.

I finished in time to hear the crackling of the speakers; my private plane was old but functional.

"This is your captain speaking, buckle up." A man of many words.

Plonking down beside Winston, I did as the captain suggested; I may be immortal, but I still got hurt. I spied how Winston wiped his hands with a wet wipe then stuck it in a little bag for discarding.

"What did you do with her body?"

"I opened the hatch while we were still over the ocean. Sharks will get to her soon enough."

"Good ol' chap." My meal had no family, and nobody would miss her. Unfortunately, in today's world we may be more connected than ever, yet some remained lonely.

We landed with a thump on the tarmac and taxied toward the private jet terminal at Cape Town International Airport. It was my first time visiting South Africa and I couldn't wait to see what it offered. I'd heard many wonderful stories about the Mother City that I had to see it for myself, even it if was only once.

As soon as the plane stopped, the pilot opened the door. I walked ahead of Winston, down the six steps, and came face-to-face with the tallest human I'd ever seen. He stood almost seven feet tall, a shaved head, and a nondescript face. He was as average as they came, apart from his height.

"Welcome, Mr. Kieran," the man said as he reached for my hand. I ignored it. He pulled back his hand and continued speaking. "I'm George, your host. How was your flight?"

"Delightful," I smirked. "Is everything in order for our travels?" I eyed Winston, letting him know they needed to be careful with my luggage. My possessions were priceless and dear to me. I wouldn't bat an eyelash killing someone if they damaged anything.

"Yes, Mr. Kieran." George snapped his fingers for the staff to unload our things while Winston barked orders at them. "They tinted the vehicle as per your request, along with reinforcement. Um," George stuttered and violently paged through a booklet. When he found what he was looking for, finally added. "There was a slight issue with your accommodation—"

"What?" I commanded, and George's cheeks reddened.

"Uhm—"

"Uhm? What is it? Spit it out, boy!"

Before, George's accent was very English—similar to those from England with a slight twist, but the more he stammered, the more his accent changed. My brows furrowed at the unfamiliar accent, yet sounding very much like Dutch.

"Isaac, kry vir my die foon."

"Why do you need to phone someone? What is wrong?" I demanded.

George stared at me with frightened brown eyes, deep lines etched between his brows. "You speak Afrikaans?"

It was my turn to frown at him. "Afrikaans? That sounded like Dutch. Aren't you descendants of the Dutch settlers here in Africa?"

George nodded. "Yes, Mr. Kieran. Afrikaans is a

daughter language of Dutch, with a few adopted words from German and Khoisan languages."

"Most impressive and beautiful, and yes, I understand your language. You were saying?"

"Right, why did I need to phone." He glanced nervously at his papers.

A sly smile crept on my face. I think the poor boy wet himself. A strange odor seemed to emanate from his direction, and I wrinkled my nose.

"They weren't able to secure the material needed for your curtains, but they installed a similar quality used in hotels, and added an extra layer for thickness."

"Right, I will see how I manage. And I'll be troubling you if it doesn't work." I glowered down at George, who swallowed hard.

Once he found his voice he added, "Yes, Mr. Kieran," he croaked, coughing into his fist. "I will see if we can source the material you need."

"Good, boy." I patted the top of his strangely shaped, bald head and headed towards the vehicle. "Come, Watson. I want to see the sights."

Winston nodded and made the attendants hurry to load our luggage in the other vehicle.

Chapter Two

DECLAN

The thirty-minute drive to the secluded and affluent Clifton suburb in Cape Town was breathtaking. The full moon splashed its silver tendrils all around us, hiding behind that gracious mountain. At four in the morning, African time, the roads were quiet with a crisp chill in the air.

The odd vehicle passed on both directions of the highway—which was on the wrong side of the road. I shook my head, these South Africans confused me. A bus with only one light and a door handle missing passed our vehicle; they were most likely employees heading to work or youngsters coming back from a club or bar.

We passed Observatory on our right with Table Mountain on our left, and the silver moon hiding behind it. Our driver, Keith, took the offramp onto Philip Kgosana Drive where we passed homes, hospitals and shopping centers.

After a bit the streetlights became less and less, the road darkened, then we went downhill. Silver light from the moon splashed across the ocean as we travelled the last stretch toward the house I'd rented for the month. Winston had made all the arrangements, to say I was inquisitive was an understatement.

Our quiet driver parked in the driveway and opened the garage door. Once it opened, he parked inside. Winston opened my door and graciously held his hand out for me to grab so I could step out comfortably.

I glanced around the garage and the size of it impressed me; one could easily fit four SUVs with room to spare.

We followed the driver through a door leading from the garage to the foyer, revealing the lavish mansion where five servants waited.

"Good evening, Mr. Kieran," said the man. His eyes flitted to Winston, who no doubt shook his head. The man kept his hands behind his back, sparing me the need to arch an eyebrow at his proffered hand. "My name is Jeff; I am your butler for the duration of your stay. This is Nancy," — he pointed to the next person, — "she ensures everything remains clean and tidy. She will do your laundry and dry cleaning, and will ensure your accommodations are spotless."

Nancy curtsied, averted her eyes like a good submissive. Her blond hair tied neatly in a bun, no makeup, and a slender figure. Awfully young though, if I had to guess she was about twenty. I already liked her.

When she glanced up at me, I winked. She blushed terribly and quickly stared at the floor.

"This is Ursula," Jeff pointed to the next lady who had curly red hair, braided neatly down her back and out of her face. Her bright green eyes filled with mystery, and although she was slightly on the whole-lot-of-woman side, she was pretty.

Ursula curtsied and stared directly into my eyes. I wondered whether she knew what vampires could do with our stares; all I had to do was say the words and she'd do it.

Winston cleared his throat, and Ursula quickly stared at my shoes.

One side of my mouth curved ever so slightly at her defiance, I liked it. She was older, perhaps thirty, maybe thirty-three. She was taller than Nancy, her chest at least a larger C-cup and all natural. I imagined sinking my teeth into those puppies and felt my pants tighten. There was no doubt Ursula saw my erection as her cheeks glowed, hiding her freckles.

"You've met Keith, your driver. We have another who rotates with Keith, and you'll meet him tomorrow when his shift starts."

There was something about Keith I couldn't quite place. He was quiet, suave—but not too much. I caught him stealing glances at Nancy. Perhaps he fancied her, or she was his girlfriend; I'd have to remedy that during my stay.

"And Simon is your chef. He has a menu planned, but you are welcome to change it."

I side glanced Winston who stepped in front of me.

"Perhaps we could have a brief chat," Winston grabbed Simon by his elbow and led him towards the kitchen.

"Allow me to show you around," Jeff offered.

I gave a curt nod and followed.

The ladies scurried away like mice while I followed Jeff around the very overpriced, but lavish mansion. I watched Jeff as he walked in front of me. He was my height, jet black hair cut short and neatly out of his face and shaved around his ears. His chiseled jaw and aquiline nose suited him; I would've thought he would be ugly with that nose, but it actually made him handsome. He wore his black slacks tight, but his black dress shirt fit nicely around his broad shoulders. He spoke about the owners of the house and their other properties in the area which they rented out while they lived in Canada. They frequented here for a months' vacation once a year.

Jeff first showed me the living area with the large glass doors that opened out to a veranda with enough seating for twenty people and a large, heated pool. The house boasted a home automation system I could program to my liking. I'd get Winston to ensure everything was closed during the day. Jeff showed how the glass doors closed and with the flick of a button the black tinting darkened the rooms—which I liked very much.

Next, we went to the six bedrooms one floor up, each with their own bathroom. They had altered the master bedroom specifically to my needs, which included thick, black curtains. They managed to acquire similar curtains to what I'd specified, which they would switch out the moment they received the ones I really wanted. For the hefty price tag I was paying, I expected nothing less.

There was a cinema, gym, and bar area. They even had a separate twin-bed spa room where Ursula doubled as the masseuse. Unless I preferred the touch of a male, then Jeff would be my go-to-guy.

I winked at him when he said that, and the man blushed salmon. I told him I had no preference, whoever was available would suffice.

"The staff sleep on the premises, in the lower level," Jeff said, pointing at the stairs near the front door that led down.

"Do you think it's fair?" I asked.

"What do you mean?"

"That someone like me, can stay here," — I lifted my arms at all the rooms, — "yet they packed the staff tightly like sardines below. Most likely similar to that on cruise ships."

Jeff blanched, and his American accent slipped. He sounded very South African as he stuttered. "No, absolutely not. It is our job, and we get paid well—"

"How often is this house rented out?"

"It's booked a year in advance."

"But you managed to squeeze us in?" Winston had contacted them two weeks ago to enquire about our stay, and they'd promptly provided us with their availability. Either Jeff was lying and it wasn't booked out for the year, or Winston was just that convincing.

"Yes, well, uh…" His accent reverted to sounding American and his cheeks their healthy shade of pink once more. He kept combing his fingers through his hair and stared nervously at me.

I grabbed the hand before he could run it through his now oily hair, stared into his lovely dark eyes and spoke. "Relax when you're around me, Jeff. Just do everything I ask, never utter a word of my wants and needs, and I'll reward you very kindly," I said in my velvety tone that made women drop their panties. "Nod if you understand."

Jeff licked his lips and nodded. His gaze slightly hazy. I let go of his hand even though his hand lingered, needed to hold on to me. When he finally let go of my fingers, he coughed into that same hand, and blinked a few times as he glanced around. Then when he saw me standing closer, he swallowed.

"Do you want me, sir? Ah… I mean, do you need anything, Mr. Kieran?"

I stifled a chuckle, but I smiled warmly. I enjoyed the company of men and women depending on my mood. Men's bodies were hard and always ready. While women's bodies were soft and delicate and always needing to wait for their flower to open for me. I shivered at the delicious thought.

"Help me with my jacket." I turned my back on Jeff. He stepped closer, and I felt his heat against my chilled body. He grabbed my collar and gently pulled off my jacket, careful not to touch me. Good boy.

"I'll just keep it here." He dashed off to hang it in the closet near the front door. He turned to look my way, his eyes large as saucers. No doubt hoping I hadn't seen the bulge in his pants. I missed nothing.

Winston entered the living area with a glass of sherry, handing it to me. "Would you like to sit by the fireplace this morning, Master?"

I took the glass out of his hand, sniffed the aroma and sipped; sweet, sharp, delectable. I nodded and followed my minion to the next room where the fire blazed.

"Please let us know if you require anything else—"

I flicked my wrist, and the door closed, abruptly ending Jeff's sentence. He was so young with much to learn. I fancied him, and only time would tell what happened during my stay.

"Are there many tourists around?" I asked as I sat in a large leather chair. It was old, but still in mint condition.

"The travel agent said few, and Simon agreed. The houses on either side are holiday rentals too. We may or may not see anybody, or we'll see a rush of beachgoers. We'll see."

I nodded my understanding and had another sip. It did nothing to me, but it helped the mundanes relax around me. It was the right color, rich, maroon, and thick; slightly chilled, although I preferred the real stuff warm and straight out the bottle.

"What time does the sun rise?" I glanced outside. The large moon splashed its silver glow against the water, animating the waves. I saw the private beach below, no doubt I had a private entrance.

"During the winter months, the sun rises just after seven."

I nodded and stared at the wicked flames in the fireplace, angry sparks doing their best to escape. In one swift motion, I stood and floated towards the door and opened it with a flick of my wrist. I stepped out onto the balcony and the sea air greeted me. The sounds of the waves were loud in the quiet night. The stars twinkled brightly, surrounding the moon in all her glory. The sun wouldn't rise for another two hours. Glancing left and right then behind me and Winston nodded—no doubt knowing my thoughts.

I levitated high above the house, ensuring none of the occupants saw me, and slowly started my descent towards the soft sand.

Turning back, the lights in the house dimmed, and I silently thanked my minion for looking after me. I drank the rest of the sherry and threw the empty glass in the ocean; a soft plonk as it struck a wave.

I removed my shoes, socks, pants and coat, followed by my shirt and entered the water. "Christ, it's cold," I mumbled to myself. As old as I was, water this freezing still struck my vampire bones. After a moment, the chill subsided, and I swam farther out.

The waves calmed my frantic mind; I had decisions to make that would change everything, hence my vacation.

After my swim, I picked up my clothing and walked towards the entrance to the house. I raised my head when a sound caught my attention; a lullaby sung by a woman with a sultry voice. I narrowed my eyes at the pathways weaving through the houses near the private beach and caught sight of her sandy brown hair, then her face as she came around the corner. I blended in with the shadows for fear of scaring her with my naked body; I didn't want my conquests frightened so soon, although it would be fun. No, I wanted to watch her. I wanted to see what she was doing at this godly hour.

The young woman glanced around nervously, much like I had done earlier, thumbed her shirt strap, and pulled it down. Her naked breasts spilled free. They were beautiful. She pulled her top down her hips and in one swift motion pulled her shorts down too.

My cock hardened at the thought of ravishing her body. But I wanted to watch her first. So instead of launching myself on her, I continued watching, and most definitely drooling.

She sauntered to the water's edge and froze the moment the cold water touched her right foot. She winced when both feet got wet followed by swear words. She shuddered as she continued walking in, then dived into the water with the next wave.

I pulled on my pants and left the rest of my clothing in a heap and sat myself down beside her clothing. She hadn't noticed me yet. I was sure she'd scream the moment she saw me gawking at her. I could always silence her quickly.

When she finished swimming, she walked slowly out with the waves, heading to her clothing. She combed her fingers through her wet hair, pulling it out of her face and squeezed the water out. The moment her eyes flitted to her clothing, and then to me, she froze.

In a moment like this I waited for the ear-piercing screams that ensured others ran to help her, but she surprised me. She just stared, possibly intrigued by the half-naked, wet man sitting near her clothing.

"A girl swimming naked by herself is a recipe for disaster." I taunted, licking my lips.

"Nobody comes here this time of the morning." She cocked her head to the side as her gaze raked up my body.

"Do you swim every day?"

"I prefer the quiet of the early morning to the busy day."

I loved night owls.

She walked towards me with a seductive smile. "Are you enjoying the show?" she asked as she picked up her shirt and slipped it on.

"Oh definitely, I think this is the best reality TV show I've ever seen."

Her smile reached her eyes as she picked up her shorts and pulled them on. Her breasts wet and shining through her thin top, teasing me. She was not a shy girl.

"I'm over there," I pointed at the mansion behind us.

Her eyes widened, then she quickly schooled her features. "Oh," she said nonchalantly. "I stay up there, with my folks."

"Do they know you come here early in the morning?"

"No," she giggled. "What fun would that be?"

I stood, pretending to struggle even though I didn't. "Declan." I proffered my hand. Usually, I hated touching humans, but this girl was different. I wanted her to touch me.

"Lana," she shook my hand, delicately yet confidently. "You're American?"

"Born and bred, and you're South African?" I reached for her face and pulled strands of hair from her cheek. She closed her eyes and swallowed hard, I smirked and neared.

Her heart raced, her chest heaved, and her hard nipples brushed against my chest through her clothing. I caught the strap of her top between my fingers and near the shell of her ear I said, "So beautiful." I trailed my finger down her collarbone, and between her breasts. Her breath hitched and her eyes shot open. I stood back and admired the trembling puddle before me.

Lana swallowed again, then started biting her bottom lip. "I... uhm," she finally said, glancing over her shoulder. There was only one other light on at a house nearby I guessed was her parent's. "Uh," she continued her stuttering.

Then the little minx caught me off guard by wrapping her arms around me, pressing her wet body against mine and pulling me down to her. The moment our lips touched I didn't hold back, I bruised her mouth with mine, and I swallowed her whimpers. I pulled her closer, one hand at the back of her head to keep her in place and the other between us as I reached between her legs. Her pants were damp against her cold, wet skin. She moaned the moment my fingers trailed between her shorts and went lower. Her mound neatly trimmed and her folds slick with desire.

But I wouldn't do her here, not like this, I wanted the privacy to taste her as I pleasured her body, and having sand caught everywhere was not fun. I slowed the kiss, her tongue tasting mine, and I removed my hand from her delicate folds. She moaned her frustrations as she regained consciousness and what I was not doing. I cupped her face to stop the kiss. But I continued staring into her emerald-colored eyes.

"Are you allowed out the house during the evenings or do you seek permission from your parents?"

"Uh," she licked her lips and cast her eyes back at the

house again. "I actually stay in my parents' guest house until I find a place of my own, so no, I don't need their permission. Anymore." Her cheeks flushed when her eyes flitted to mine once more.

"Come to this house," — I pointed at the rental mansion again, — "tonight at nine."

"Okay," she rocked onto her toes and kissed me chastely. "See ya later." She skipped like a schoolgirl back to the house with the bright light. She opened a side gate and slipped out of sight.

I didn't know what it was about Lana, but she intrigued me. She was young, possibly mid-twenties, with a very naughty streak. And I'd love to taste it.

Once I was back inside my suite, I enjoyed a hot shower. My clothing already packed in the closet and my bathrobe set out on the bed. I dried and pulled my robe against my body, tying it in front.

"Have you eaten Watson?" I asked.

He grunted at my name calling again, but answered, anyway. "Yes, behind the house are woods where wild animals roam; tonight, I had a wild hare."

I arched a dark eyebrow. "Wild hare? Are you even full with that measly snack? God, look at you. You could easily eat a deer without coming up for air." Winston was on the short side, but incredibly strong and built like an ox. When he shaved his hair like now, one hardly noticed it was red, unless he grew a beard—which, thank heavens, he shaved before our trip. And he no longer shuffled now that we were safely on land.

"Yes, well, I'd rather not draw attention to us and certainly not so early in our stay." That was a low jab from him. He obviously saw my interaction with Lana.

"She's coming over tonight at nine, ensure there are

refreshments for our guest. The sun will rise soon, and I'll be dead to the world. As always, nobody may enter here while I sleep."

"Yes, Master. If that's all, then I shall retire myself."

Winston picked up the remote, pressed a button, and the smart glass changed to black, and the thick blinds closed. He then closed the additional black curtains I'd asked them to install, just in case some idiot played with the remote and opened the windows in my room. I was not a day walker and would burn to dust if that enormous ball of fire touched my skin.

I locked the door after Winston left, removed my robe and climbed under the satin sheets, cool and smooth against my naked body. The moment I felt my body weigh down, I knew the sun was rising, and I died.

Chapter Three

DECLAN

The next evening Keith brought us to Cape Town Waterfront. The road he drove on was scenic along the coast through Sea Point, Green Point and then the Waterfront.

The smell of fish assaulted my nostrils as the wind whipped across the waves, spraying light mist along the seawall. The Waterfront's bright lights felt surreal as more people approached the busy mall.

In the distance was Table Mountain. The atmosphere of just standing here, casting my eyes at the sights, was something I'd never experienced before. It did however remind me of the time I went to Dubai where there's ocean, sand, heat, and modern skyscrapers alight with colors. But the Mother City air was different; the various smells of ocean, food, sweets, and lust filled my nostrils, and I couldn't wait to see what else it had to offer.

Instead of going through the mall and sea of bodies, I headed toward the Clock Tower while Winston tended to some shopping. He was worse than a woman addicted to buying stuff. I rolled my eyes when he just about squealed when he saw the For Sale signs.

I left Winston to do his thing and crossed the V&A Waterfront Swing Bridge, heading toward the Clock Tower and the various shops surrounding it. On the opposite side stood another building for one of the more popular banks with various hidden passages and dark corners. There used to be a Ripley's Believe It or Not shop, but it had closed. In the corner stood a lady-of-the-night, my favorite, while I her hunter-of-the-night.

A security guard watched me intently; arched eyebrow, thick lips in a tight line and dark beady eyes on me. Then I realized his face remained in that state at every passerby. Three children distracted him, threatening to drop ice cream everywhere while their parents tried desperately to get them away from the Lindt chocolate store. I pitied the fool who had children; they were vile and needy creatures. Ick.

A sound caught my attention. I turned to face her, a smile splitting my face in two. With a finger, she beckoned me closer; a keen sense of smell for the money in my pocket. Her dark eyes luring me to her dark web. I obliged and followed her.

I asked for her rate, which was extremely cheap considering the Rand-Dollar exchange rate. I handed over the notes; she gasped, stating it was too much. And before her suspicion overruled her emotions, I pushed her farther into the dark corner and covered her screams with my larger hand. Her caramel-colored skin radiant and enticing. Her scent years at this job, but I didn't want what was between her legs. I wanted what coursed through her veins. The delicious red juice that made my mouth salivate.

"It's going to be fine, my dear. I will not hurt you. I give you my word," I said. My tone velvety smooth as she nodded her understanding and started to relax, no longer needing to scream for help. I removed my hand from her mouth as she continued to stare at me, lost within my dark eyes.

My fangs elongated, my hunger stirred, and I bit into my dinner. I hummed my pleasure as she sank against my body, no longer able to fight against the numbness shooting down every limb. My bite was potent; it never hurt, but it never pleasured either. My bite filled with venom, making my victims numb. If I wasn't careful, I'd kill.

Her sweet blood hot and delicious going down my throat. I wanted more but I'd stop. I pulled away before her heart gave in. I never killed ladies-of-the-night; they had an important job, and they did it well. And I always paid enough. She could go straight home and recover from a bout of the flu for a couple of days.

Carefully, I laid her against the floor of the dark alley and slipped two more notes into the pocket near her breast so her Manager couldn't take his share while she recovered.

I slipped through the alleys, back over the swing bridge and met up with Winston where our driver waited.

Full, happy, and horny; I was ready for my date with Lana.

Chapter Four

URSULA

The vampire crossed the swing bridge, and I ran after him, ensuring I didn't lose him again among the sea of bodies. He was a zippy American bastard who had caught my attention years ago. I needed to watch him in his natural habitat—in the dark shadows.

After monitoring his actions from afar and for so long, I had to get closer when I heard he was finally coming to my country. I had to keep watch over him while he was here. I'd researched many supernatural's, but Declan was the one who had caught my eye and I needed to know everything about him.

I watched him stalk towards the shadows, focused and unrelenting. An exceptional vampire who made my heart stutter in my chest, and desire bloom in my core. All I wanted was one taste, one night with him, to sate my appetite. To feel his cold, hard body pressed against mine. I shuddered at the yummy thought. If others knew about my desires, they'd think I lost my mind, but I was sane and pursued the night hunter.

Just when I thought I'd lost him, I heard children screaming, ice cream falling and the security guard yelling. But there was something else. The hairs on my forearms stood up, making me shiver.

To my right, I heard it. I narrowed my eyes toward the dark shadows. My heart raced while my breath caught in my chest. If he caught me watching, he would kill me for sure. I needed to play this carefully.

I hid near the now vacant shop and carefully walked along the dark wall.

He moved in the shadows; I caught his coat billowing as he moved. I stepped closer. His hand was over her mouth while his other kept her body up.

My chest rose and fell as I watched. I felt like a mouse caught in his trap.

She lay limp against him, unseeing and unmoving. I wondered what his bite felt like as I reached for my neck, craving his touch. I desperately wanted this. I wanted him. But… what if… then again, my what ifs usually ended badly. The risk of him killing me was great. I liked my life. Well… not really, but it was mine to ruin as I saw fit. And I wanted to do this. I needed to do it.

Slowly he sat her down, fixed the hair he ruffled and added more notes in her secret breast pocket. He was forever the gentleman.

I squeezed between the two brick buildings as he passed. I'd wait a few minutes before heading back to my car then back to work where I'd bump into him again. And I couldn't wait.

The woman on the floor stirred as she slowly awoke, a smile flirted across her face even though it was marked with confusion. She probably knew she encountered a john but wouldn't remember what had happened. She touched the side of her neck where he'd punctured her skin. And I cursed myself for not bringing my camera. I pulled out my cellphone, removed the flash and filmed her recovery.

A blast of wind slapped me in the face, and I almost dropped my phone. The woman shrieked. I corrected my hand to record her again.

A dark figure loomed over her, abruptly picked her up, nestled his face on the other side of her body and bit into her. She cried as she tried to move but was incapable. He shoved his hand down her throat to silence her, breaking her jaw. Her eyes bugged as her arms lay limply at her sides. He pulled her head from her neck, then devoured her insides greedily.

I whimpered and covered my hand over my mouth. Tears streamed down my face. Everything happened so quickly. The thing was swift, dangerous, and in an instant gone. Wind blasted past me again as I steadied my phone. It left behind a mangled mess. Her insides were outside and her head barely on her shoulders. But the bite of the vampire remained visible for authorities to see.

Chapter Five

LANA

I downed a shot of tequila before walking towards the house Declan had pointed to in the early hours of the morning.

My mind reeled with what he'd done to my body and felt my neck and cheeks heat. My mother would turn in her grave if she knew what had happened. How his hand trailed under my shorts and to my... I squirmed just thinking about him.

But... there was something about him I couldn't deny. I'd dated guys, partied, but none of them ever came close to this guy. He was at least a head taller. His toned body perfectly sculptured as if carved from marble. His high cheekbones and dark, piercing blue eyes sent molten desire spreading through my veins.

Oh my gods, his eyes; they were so blue they reminded me of the ocean on hot summer days when I could see to the bottom of the seafloor. I craved for his week-old stubble across his chiseled jaw to scratch my chin while we kissed, and I combed my fingers through his dark hair. A nervous giggle tore through my lips and I shook the fantasy away. Maybe, just maybe, it might finally happen.

If anyone asked if I'd seen anyone perfect, I would've said no, but Declan was near perfect. He came across as confident and dangerous, but he hid his sensitive nature, although I had a small glimpse of it this morning when he didn't take full advantage of me. Even though I would've allowed him to. Who would've thought I'd have a one-night stand? Certainly not me.

Unfortunately, as handsome as he was, he most likely had a string of women and I just a notch on his belt. I wasn't going into this completely blind or naïve, I was flirting with desire and the danger thrilled me.

I shrugged as I climbed the many steps to the mansion and saw the large pool. I bent down and felt the water; it was warm and inviting. I stood and swallowed my tongue when I caught sight of the inside of the place. High ceiling, luxurious furniture, and artwork adorned the walls. My stepmother had told us about the owners, but I'd never seen the inside.

As tempting as Declan was. I felt like a small animal walking into the lion's den. But being curious by nature, I wanted to see where this would go and crossed the threshold.

"Hi," I said. "Uh—" I swallowed my words when a muscular man my height entered the room and smiled. He had shaved red hair and piercing green eyes. Was this his boyfriend? I felt utterly confused.

"Declan will be with you shortly. Would you like a drink while you wait?"

"Sure."

Make that two, I have nerves that required calming. I thought as I entered the massive living area.

I thought our house was big, but this one was four times the size. When my dad married his second wife after my mom passed away, we moved in with her, into her house. It was her money. She didn't want me living with her and made a guest room on top of her garage for me; which suited me just fine. The less I saw of her, the better. If we had a house as big as this one, I'd never see them.

Declan traversed the stairs like he was parading for the queen, and I almost laughed.

"My name is Winston," the man I'd greeted earlier said, and offered me a drink. "I hope you drink apple martinis?"

"Sure, thanks. I'm Lana." I proffered my hand. He took my hand in both of his and shook. His hands were warm and didn't linger. At first glance he seemed rough around the edges, but he made me feel welcomed. I beamed at him, and his smile brightened his pleasant face.

Declan cleared his throat as he stood in the entrance.

I frowned. *What was he waiting for?*

Winston ran to his side, Declan whispered near his ear. Winston turned towards me, his demeanor changed, making me flinch. I didn't know what Declan said, but it left me feeling tense.

"Dinner is ready, please call if you need anything else." Winston bowed low, dipped his head towards me and scurried away.

"What was that about? Isn't he joining us?"

"Who? Watson? Heavens no. He's my…" — he waved his hand in the air, — "personal assistant."

"Winston."

"What?"

"His name is Winston." The lines between my eyes deepened. If Winston was his personal assistant, he should know his name.

"How is your apple martini?"

"Fine." I had another small sip.

"Good." He nodded and closed the gap. "How was the rest of your day? Did you do anything interesting?"

"I worked." And thumbed behind me. "I'm a part-time accountant for an insurance company—"

"Ah." He raised his chin. "What do you do for fun?"

"There are places one can go depending on what you like."

"And what do you like?"

I swallowed hard, unable to read his features. An uneasiness settled within my bones; one I hadn't had this morning when we first met. Declan seemed determined to know everything about me in a short amount of time. It's as if he had a time limit. I didn't like it. He also stared at me like I was his meal. I hated that.

"I have packed away your clothing, Mr. Kieran," a woman said as she entered. She wore a uniform, her eyes twinkled with youth and her blond hair in a neat ponytail.

"That will be all." He dismissed her with a flick of his hand.

When another man entered asking whether he needed to go anywhere. Declan yelled at him, and that we were not to be disturbed.

I didn't appreciate how he treated those who worked for him. Unaware of the full extent of their working conditions but Declan was rude and heartless. I'd been on the receiving end of a tyrant before, and it's unpleasant. People like him had a way of making you feel insignificant and worthless.

I wasn't sure what it was, but this Declan was different to the one I'd met this morning. This was probably the side of him he hid away. I didn't like this Declan one bit. He may be handsome, and I was sure he was outstanding in other areas, but he was cruel. No matter what my intentions were before, I'd lost my appetite, and no longer wished to stay here.

Declan approached. There was something about the way he stared at me, making me swallow hard.

I stepped backward until my head collided with a painting on the wall. Before Declan reached me, I ducked out of his embrace.

He glowered, quickly schooled his features and tugged on his shirt, neatening it. He leaned against the tabletop and folded his arms.

"Would you like to eat?" he asked nonchalantly like he didn't scare me a second ago.

"No, this was a mistake. I'm going home. Thanks for the drink." I placed the glass on the table and headed for the stairs leading towards the beach.

"Why? I thought you wanted me," he said in a soft, delicious tone that made the hairs on my neck stand up. He rushed to my side, slipped an arm around my waist and pulled me against him. His eyes darkened as he stared at me while rage filled my veins. I felt his erection dig into me which only made matters worse.

I pushed against his hard chest to get out of his grip. When he didn't let go, I slapped him. His eyes glowed. I gasped. He stepped back and so did I. My foot caught and I tripped, landing in the pool. When I came up for air, he held out a hand with a towel in the other.

"Get away from me!" I yelled, ignoring him and the towel, and climbed the steps out of the pool.

"Don't go," he pleaded, following closely behind me. "At least stay for dinner."

I ignored him. Before I headed in the stairs direction, I turned around and shoved a finger in his chest. "I don't know what's wrong with you, maybe it's your entitled demeanor, but I don't appreciate how you treat others or how you make me feel. You're an arsehole. No amount of money will make you a better person. I don't like the way you spoke to your employees, nor do I like how you stare at me. You're a predator. Now get away from me."

"Lana?" said a familiar voice.

I peered around Declan and saw Ursula.

"Ursula? Do you work here?"

Ursula nodded and closed the gap. "What's going on?" She glared up at Declan, arching an eyebrow.

Declan got the hint and stepped away. When I glanced at him, something flashed in his eyes, something akin to regret. A flurry of emotions crossed his face that left my heart beating in its cage, and guilt flooded me. If he thought his behavior impressed me, he was mistaken.

"Did he hurt you? Why are you wet?" Ursula asked, fussing over me.

"It's fine. It was a misunderstanding, and I was just leaving." I hugged Ursula, apologized for making her wet, and we descended the stairs. "We haven't spoken in ages, perhaps we can catch up sometime?" I said as I walked away.

"I'd like that. My number hasn't changed," Ursula said, staying on the last step.

"Great, chat later," I yelled as I ran down the path.

I felt like Cinderella leaving the ball, only I wasn't in love with the prince, and would much rather enjoy the company of my stepmother than remain in his broody company.

Chapter Six

DECLAN

"You know Lana?" I asked the redhead.

"What did you do to her?"

"I asked you first."

"Nah-hah, mister, answer me. What did you do to her? She looked like you assaulted her. And why was she in the pool?" Ursula demanded, resting her hands on her hips, and tapped her foot.

I exhaled and sat on the nearest chair. I ruined all chances with a woman I really liked. Here I was thinking I was holding it together, playing it smooth—but... obviously I wasn't.

"Well?" Ursula demanded.

The little spitfire stood in front of me, hands still on her hips and her lips in a tight line. I could always bite her, make her numb. I shook my head, expelling the thought.

"I messed up okay—"

"What did you do?"

"Nothing, I didn't lay a finger on her. But," — I shrugged, — "I may have been rude."

"She doesn't like arseholes."

"You mean assholes."

She frowned at me. "Whatever. The spelling differs, but it still means the same. Which means you," — she shoved two fingers into my sternum, — "are one of them."

I held up my hands in surrender and glanced in the direction Lana had disappeared. She was different. She stood her ground and challenged me. No matter what I offered, she had integrity, and I messed up any chance I had with her.

"Help me win her back."

"What? Are you nuts? You've had your chance with her. It's over before it even began." Ursula stood between my legs, nudging them apart. I shot a confused look at her. Now she wore a smirk on her face; a very naughty smirk.

"If this is some game you're playing—"

"No." She shook her head.

"Then what are you doing?"

In one swift motion Ursula straddled me, cupped my face and kissed me. Her tongue teased the opening of my lips, and I opened my mouth. I rarely rejected advances, and Ursula was persistent. Our tongues tasting the other. Her lips soft and delicate. Her hands mussed my hair while I squeezed her waist.

When she'd finished assaulting my mouth, she sat back, her eyes still closed, and licked her lips.

"Um, that was delicious. But…" she climbed off me, dusting down her skirt. When her green eyes found mine, she smiled. "Thank you. I'll never forget that Declan." When she saw the confusion on my face she added, "Haven't you ever wanted someone so badly that when opportunity knocks, you'd jump at the chance? Or jump on their lap?" She grinned and didn't wait for my reply when she continued speaking. "Well, I've wanted to kiss you for a very long time. I needed to scratch that itch and taste you. I can tell a lot by the way someone kisses, and you're not bad, but…" she shrugged. "I like you, but you're not the one for me. And I promise. It will only be this once. My lips are sealed." She pretended to lock her mouth with an imaginary key and tucked the key in her pocket for safekeeping. "I'll help you get Lana. I doubt she'll want you after how you behaved tonight, but we can try. Oh, and don't tell Jeff."

The lines between my eyes deepened. "You're with Jeff?" She nodded. "But he's gay?"

She harrumphed, deep in thought.

Jeff was delicious and came in a tight package. It left me curious as to her relationship with him.

"Well, shit." She sat and fixed her shirt. "That explains a lot. We've only slept together like four times the last six months. I thought he might be gay, but I wasn't sure, you know. Not that it matters but it would've been nice to know so I could handle situations a bit better. Then again I hadn't bothered to ask him—"

"Don't be so hard on yourself, he's in denial. It's not your fault. He needs to decide what he wants and come out of the proverbial closet."

"Well, I think he wants you. He couldn't stop talking about you when we got into bed yesterday." She frowned. "Or rather, this morning. Anyway, he's still an awesome guy and I'll always love him." Then she stared at me with enormous eyes and gasped. "I need to show you something."

"You mean apart from the inside of your mouth." I chuckled lightheartedly and stood, following her inside.

She slapped my chest as she ran past. "No silly, I just wanted to test drive those full lips for myself. And sorry, as lovely as you are, I'm just not into you. Shu, I'm relieved now that it's out." She said, disappearing, then ran back with her cellphone in her hand and raised her other hand. "Before you get your panties in a knot, or rather… never mind. I know what you are." She stared at me, silently conversing with me. "You're a night hunter. Your staple diet comprises vital fluids," she whispered.

The breath I didn't need caught in my throat. It wasn't a secret vampires roamed the streets, yet her knowing I was one left me on edge. There were things she was keeping secret, and I needed to understand more.

"What exactly does that mean?" I had to ask. I contemplated draining her then throwing her body in the ocean or I could wait until she showed me what she had on her cellphone?

"That you're a vampire."

"No, I'm not."

She placed a hand on her hips and arched an eyebrow, letting me know she knew I was lying.

"Whatever, okay, don't be angry, but I have a website dedicated to you." When she saw my expression, the one I kept for enemies, she rocked onto her toes and kissed me chastely, knocking the anger right out of me. "I'm your number one fan, dummy." She slapped my chest again.

"Just stop hitting me." I rubbed my chest. "Now, tell me what you're going on about."

"Right, so you're a vampire, and I've been following anything and everything about you since forever. I built this website dedicated to you and your travels, and especially what they want you to do."

She closed the gap, shoving her shoulder under my arm so I could hold her. She was a strange little creature. I didn't know if I liked or despised her, especially since she knew what I was. She flicked to a website on her cellphone that read, *'The Master Vampire everybody wants to know.'*

"I get about two-thousand hits a day, and with the number of ads I make enough to live comfortably. Jeff knows a ton of people and the owners of this house. He got us both jobs here when I asked him nicely." She batted her eyelashes; that's probably how she got her way. "When I heard you were heading this way," she shrugged, "I had to do everything in my power to meet you." Her eyes glistened in the dim light, and I couldn't help but smile at my first groupie. "But something happened after you left tonight. Someone followed you." Her words sobered me.

"You saw?"

She nodded. "Someone killed the woman you left alive seconds later. I don't know what it was—"

I grabbed the phone out of her hands and watched the video. The demon approached, sucked the woman dry, disemboweled and killed her. Leaving her neck exposed. And ultimately leaving evidence that I was there.

"Someone wants to frame you for her murder, or some-thing," Ursula said, leaving my cold body chilled. "Can they do that if they only have your bite marks?"

I shook my head. Our bite marks were not in a directory with a picture of our faces since nobody could take a vampire's photograph. But this little spitfire had video evidence of me drinking from a woman and could use it against me if she chose to.

"What do you want?"

"I want to be with you. No, that came out wrong, I don't want you—you. I want you to turn me and I want to work with you."

"No," I shook my head, "I don't turn humans."

She grabbed her phone. Tears welled in her eyes and her bottom lip trembled. "Please. You're all I have left."

"Christ, you're needy."

"Master?" Winston said. My trusty minion rescuing me. "Give her what she wants. She means you no harm." He raised his hand toward her and nodded. "She's being honest and wants to help you."

"This doesn't concern you, Watson."

"But it does," he said gravely. He was right; I needed vampires in my kiss, but I didn't want to make them.

"Did you know about this?" I pointed at the cellphone.

"No," he shook his head. "But I heard her pleas. This is what she wants, and no doubt thought hard about her decision. She has done so much and only wants a chance."

"If I figure out who this is. Will you do it? Will you turn me and make me part of your kiss?" she asked but kept her gaze on Winston.

I sighed. Winston nodded curtly with a raised eyebrow. His little warning to me. Yes, I was his master, but we were more like partners. The only difference I hardly treated him with respect.

"First you kiss me, then you blackmail me—"

"No," she shook her head, "it's not blackmail, I promise. It's a kind request. Please. Jeff is gay, my parents are dead, and there's nothing for me here. Nothing. You're literally my last hope. Please," she begged—her big green eyes pleading.

I hated when women begged.

"Let's first see who it is. Okay. Then we can talk some more."

Ursula squealed with delight, pecked my cheek then ran and pecked Winston's cheek who blushed from her affection. She stared at him a heartbeat too long, refusing to let go of his shoulders, then eventually she pulled herself away from him, disappearing down to her accommodation.

"Master," Winston said, bowing low.

"Watson," I yelled just to piss him off.

He arched an eyebrow, but his mouth curved slightly at the sides. I was glad I amused him still. The man was an insightful creature who always got on my nerves.

"I'll wake you with your rations," he said and disappeared to his room.

Chapter Seven

DECLAN

I swam over a wave, the sea water a welcomed chill against my body. I needed to collect my thoughts about what had happened with Lana, or rather what didn't happen. Lana challenged me, and I acted like an asshole. These days women didn't swoon the moment a vampire walked into the room, I had to work harder than I used to. If she was special enough, she was worth it. And Lana was.

And then there was Ursula's request following our intense kiss. The red-headed minx wanted to join my kiss, but I didn't turn humans. Not after that one time.

I rubbed my temples. I'd never had a headache before because of two women, yet here I was floating over the waves trying to figure out what had just happened and how to move forward.

Not only had I two women to figure out, but I had a demon hot on my heels. I sighed. As if I didn't have enough problems of my own.

The moon had started losing its shape as the nights

progressed to the next phase. I had until the new moon to give my answer; to accept the title of Master Vampire of Krystal Creek or to bow down low, very—very low, to the next vampire in line—the vampire I had turned and regretted. I hated him. He became a tyrant the moment he tasted blood and had been scratching at my heels ever since. I wanted to become Master Vampire of Krystal Creek, but I didn't want him part of my kiss. But somehow, he'd convinced the Council that should I reject their offer, he'd take my place.

That's why I was here. I needed a break—which was unheard of. Vampires did not need to take breaks. Perhaps it was just an excuse I used to come here for the sightseeing. I exhaled the breath I didn't need, but it was a welcome distraction.

I swam out with the waves and turned toward the dark houses, confirming I was the only one awake. My eyes flitted to the monster mansion we had rented and noted Winston standing on the balcony with a drink in his hand. He tipped his head, set his empty glass on the table and stripped off his clothing. He headed towards the trees behind the house —no doubt to catch his wild hare. The wolf needed something a little bigger, otherwise he'd be hunting little hares every evening.

When Winston asked if I was ready to speak with the Council, I'd suggested tomorrow, rather. I wasn't in the mood for their mind games. I exhaled sharply and swam back to the private beach.

I walked out of the water and combed my fingers through my wet hair and out of my face. When I spotted the familiar face, I froze. She sat on my clothing and didn't budge. I waited for her to notice me and run away. But she didn't run away when her eyes finally landed on mine, only her cheeks heated. Her lips curved upward at the corners as her eyes raked over my naked body, no doubt giving me a taste of my own medicine. Objectification was real.

"I thought you'd run away the moment you saw me?" I closed the gap between us. Being a vampire with centuries' worth of practice left me extremely comfortable naked. Standing before her, my cock twitching as I thought of ways to pleasure her.

Lana averted her eyes and stood quickly, brushing sand from her clothing, and stepped away from me.

I picked up my pants and slipped them on.

"I was thinking about that," she said. "I enjoyed the Declan I spoke to yesterday morning, not the one I spoke to in the evening. Maybe it's the six-bedroom house you're in when it's only you and your manservant."

"It's Winston's fault, he chose it." I pulled on my shirt. Lana watched me intently. "It is rather big, isn't it? Or is it you feel threatened by the money, and the possibility of power I may or may not have."

"Perhaps both," she shrugged, taking another step away from me. "It's also the way you speak to others."

Lana was right. Sometimes I spewed words without thinking. And Ursula was correct in her assessment. Lana didn't deserve my punishment. She shouldn't want me. It was best if she didn't taste the forbidden fruit. I would only hurt her. I would numb her when I drank from her neck and the possibility of killing her was real, or worse, I'd break her fragile heart.

Lana was bright eyed and wonderful. She glowed with youth and had her life ahead of her. I would only taint her. To me, she seemed like someone who loved with every inch of her body, her soul, and her mind. I could only offer her my body. The underworld had my soul, and my mind played dangerous games. My body I'd offer gladly but again, some human women wanted your heart before they bed you. I had no heart to give. It stopped beating centuries ago.

Lana smiled sadly, stepping closer. She raised her arm and with the index finger of her right hand caressed her bottom lip. I'd love nothing more than to hold her hands above her head, suck on her bottom lip then bruise her mouth with mine.

Her green eyes twinkled. Her body betrayed her as I sucked in air over my teeth. I smelled her; her scent, her fear, and her arousal.

Lana was unsure of me, but curious enough to stay. She wanted to know more. To her I was a mysterious wealthy man that sent her heart racing, even though she hated the idea of power.

I listened to the rhythm of her heart slamming against her ribs, watching her chest rising and falling. A scared little mouse.

I should hurt her now before she fell too deeply.

"Your instincts were right, Lana. You should stay away from me," I said sternly.

She flinched at the sudden shift in my mood and dropped her arm to her side.

"I will only hurt you. Find yourself a boy your age. I'm far too old and experienced for you. I will crush you." My jaw ticked as I fought for control. It felt wrong speaking to her that way, but I had to. I had to let her go.

She swallowed hard and averted her eyes. When she raised her head to look at me, her eyes welled with unshed tears. She stepped closer. I shook my head.

"I will hurt you. Get away from me."

She didn't leave. She wanted me as much as I wanted her. The only difference was, I would leave her scarred.

"I'm a bad man, Lana."

She burned my chest with her heated palm; I closed my eyes and savored her touch. Her hand moved, snaking around my neck until both arms held me and pressed her warm body against mine.

"There's something wrong with me. My instincts scream at me to run far away from you. I know you're bad. You scare the crap out of me, but..." I felt her shake her head. "You are not like the others, Declan." The way she whispered my name sent forbidden fire through my veins, warming me. I opened my eyes. "But I can't stop thinking about you, and my body remains. I can't go. Why do you think that is?"

"You're a silly girl?" I finally found the nerve to touch the curve of her hips and the swell of her ass.

"That was a rhetorical question." She giggled.

I had to stop touching her. She needed to forget about me. My dark, vile soul would corrupt someone so pure and innocent. "Well, you still needed to hear it." With all the strength I could muster, I grasped her wrists and pushed her away from me. "Go home, Lana," I said gravely as I walked past her. "Trust your instincts. Go!"

I left her standing on the beach staring wide eyed.

I didn't glance over my shoulder. I didn't want her thinking I wanted her... even though I did. It was safer that way. It was safer for her.

I passed Winston as I headed towards my room. His muzzle soaked with blood and bits of fur.

"Excellent decision, Master," he mumbled through his deformed mouth, but I understood wolf-boy.

"Good night, Watson. Sleep well."

He growled and ran past me to his room. I pressed the button and the house automatically closed in on itself. Just as the shades lowered, I saw her standing there. Still watching.

Chapter Eight

DECLAN

As I pulled on my dress shirt to fasten the cufflinks, Ursula burst through the door like a hurricane. Her curly red hair in a high ponytail, the top button of her uniform in the wrong buttonhole, and her skirt askew.

"Declan, you must see this," she said as she aimed the universal remote at the wall. The sound of cogs and pulleys filled the room as the wall moved and a secret compartment revealed a flatscreen television.

I shook my head; humans and their toys.

The screen blinked to life and a news reporter stood in the area where I'd tasted my delicious caramel darling. Even though I had left her alive, she lay slaughtered on the concrete like waste. Luckily, they'd covered her corpse so nobody could see the destruction.

I grabbed the remote from Ursula and increased the sound. "'...*a young woman found early this morning by the bank's security guard phoned the police. We believe an animal viciously attacked and mauled...*'" I switched it off.

"They killed her to get my attention," I said gravely.

They'd hurt an innocent woman for naught. Any vicious attack was usually blamed on animals. It's not like they had a database with all the types of bites. We were impossible to catalogue. "Show me the video again. But on there," I pointed at the larger screen.

"Sure," Ursula said, searching for the video on her phone. When she found what she was looking for, she pressed buttons on the remote and the video played on the big screen.

I watched again as the dark figure loomed over her, then abruptly picked her up. He shoved his face on the other side of her head, biting into her. Her spine-chilling cries made me swallow hard. Then the demon shoved his hand down her throat, silencing her, and breaking her jaw. Thank heavens they didn't show her corpse on the news. It was gruesome. The finale showed the demon pulling her head from her neck and devouring her insides.

"Not even I would…" Winston started to say when his eyes caught Ursula staring at him.

"I don't know what you are, but you aren't a vampire."

I sighed. "Just tell her before she kisses you too."

She stuck her tongue out at me. Then gave Winston all her attention. I stepped back to watch the fireworks.

"I'm a—"

"Watson is a dog."

Ursula grabbed the pillow from the couch and threw it at me. "No, he's not. Tell me. And you shush." She pointed a finger at me.

"A werewolf." Winston cleared his throat.

"That's amazing. Do you only change at full moon?"

"No, luckily not. I'm not drawn to it like the others. A witch cursed me."

"Oh, why?"

"That story is for another day, Goldilocks. Listen, did you find anything about demons causing havoc in your country?"

"Since I didn't have to work this morning, I did some digging," — she grinned, most likely because I was asleep and Winston didn't need her to do anything, — "and from what I found, demons are tricky bastards. But there have been no reported sightings on the supernatural channels I follow."

"Yes, that's all fascinating," I groaned. "Demons can move between worlds rather quickly. Apart from the demon who killed the woman, were there any stories of women waking up naked in bed, or someone doing stuff they didn't remember doing?"

"Oh." She shook her head. "No, nothing like that."

"Okay, you're not helping. The only way to lure it out is with bait. We need to make sure it follows me when I feed tonight. And Winston, you'll have to hang around. I'm going to need your furry muscle for this one."

Chapter Nine

DECLAN

Not wanting to draw attention to the place we rented, Winston had arranged for a night tour at the Kirstenbosch botanical gardens without a guide. And he hired a woman for me to feast on since the demon was intent on framing me. The least I could do was eat before the demon arrived.

The escort arrived with her large bodyguard; his shirt straining against his beefy muscles. I raised both eyebrows at Ursula when I caught her staring at him. There was no doubt he would smother the redhead with his body, but she seemed to enjoy the view.

"Behave yourself. You're drooling while I'm the one who's supposed to have dinner."

"I'm only looking." Ursula feigned innocence. "Besides, does she know what you're going to do?" she whispered.

I grinned at her and pulled a face. "Watch and learn, baby fledgling."

Winston paid the beefy guard, who nodded his approval and released his merchandise in my capable hands.

The tall, busty blond slipped her thin arm through mine

and smiled sweetly. Her perfume flooded my senses, making my eyes water. She knew what I wanted and had agreed, anyway.

Supernatural's were everywhere and didn't need to hide. But that didn't mean I wanted everybody to know my business. I had centuries of hiding in the shadows and still preferred the thrill of enjoying my meal in scandalous conduct. Knowing I could drink from her neck out in the open with nobody around to stop me sent a thrilling shiver up my spine. Except this time I might encounter the demon.

We walked towards the start of the Centenary Tree Canopy Walkway, informally called 'The Boomslang' (meaning tree snake). It's a low-impact sculptural raised walkway that wound and dipped its way through and over the trees of the botanical garden; the view was spectacular. We had the mountain behind us, the twinkling city lights before us, with the ocean in the distance.

My luscious dinner kept her arm entwined with mine and rested her head on my shoulder as we cast our eyes upon the views. The smell of fast-food and fire wafted in the air, leaving me ravenous.

"You are aware of my... tastes?"

"Uh-huh, for an extra thousand you paid, you can have anything, baby," she purred.

"I only want a taste," I whispered and turned to face her.

I cupped my dinner's face, and she instantly relaxed. She stared up at me with hooded honey-colored eyes, her eyeliner a little too thick. She was beautiful without the makeup, but no doubt her *manager* had dressed her.

My right hand slipped behind her head while my other wound around her waist and pulled her closer. Her heart rate increased, no doubt thrilled about her encounter with me, but also scared—a natural response.

My nostrils flared as I breathed in her scent; this was my favorite part. They were excited, but terrified. The conundrum made their blood pump quicker and tasted sweeter.

I never hurt, I made them numb. But it was the demon who'd be coming after us that I wanted. We would ensure her safety.

I neared the pulsing vein in her neck, her perfume no longer an issue, and kissed the spot.

She whimpered as she clutched onto my body.

The heat from her breasts a comfort. As fake as they were, I still enjoyed the view. Her low V-neck dress the color of her blood. My lips twitched the moment I kissed her neck. I opened my mouth, my fangs elongated, and I plunged into my dinner; her blood hot and delicious.

My bite numbed her within seconds, her arms fell away from my body and limply against her sides. She moaned as I bit down harder, savoring her essence. I swallowed more than I should've, but it was so hard to stop sometimes.

I squeezed her head with my right hand, and my left hand gripped her waist. She gasped the moment I unlatched myself from her skin. I licked the punctured wounds, stopping the blood flow, and licked it one more time to help with the healing.

I called for her manager to fetch her before I dropped her. He sprinted onto the canopy and picked her up.

I nodded my silent thanks.

I heard something behind me.

The manager left. I reluctantly followed. I'd much rather be staring at the view, but I had a demon to kill.

I heard a loud grunt followed by a scream.

Winston ran towards the couple as I reached the end of the canopy. The girl was gone.

"He's out," Winston said near the manager's unconscious body, sniffed the air and pointed. "They went that way." He morphed into his glorious wolf form and ran up ahead. "They dropped her over here. She's breathing," he said behind a bush.

Sounds continued behind me as something else ran on the canopy towards me.

"Declan," Ursula whispered and beckoned me with her hands. "There's something behind you," she said as she pointed her cellphone in the canopy's direction.

"Stay in the shadows." I shooed her away and stood back.

The sounds continued. It was running, galloping on the canopy. The black thing slammed into me with such force, it knocked the stale air out of my lungs. It was lightning fast and heavy as it pushed its shoulder into my sternum. Thank goodness I no longer needed my breath. It dug its talons into my ribs; I roared in pain as my claws extended and I shoved them into any parts that were soft.

Screeching sounded behind me. Another black blur slammed into us, and we tumbled to the wet grass. The new demon raised its talons, gripping my neck while I stopped its other hand from reaching the other side. It wanted to rip my head off.

I roared and slashed at the first demon, fiery liquid squirted over my hand, and it let me go. It roared in pain when I pushed my claws into its side.

The second demon flashed its red eyes, opened its mouth revealing sharp pointy teeth and rancid breath. It was about to sink its vile mouth into my neck. I let go of the first demon, swiveled around and slammed my claw into the second one, puncturing its abdomen. Thick, vile smelling blood gushed over my hand. Its ear-shattering shrill made me want to cower, but I dared not let go.

The first demon slammed its shoulder into me. A low growl sounded behind me. The first demon disappeared as my wolf took him off me, removing a limb while doing so; I'd thank him if we survived.

The second demon shrilled again. I elbowed its jaw, breaking it upon contact. With my other hand I slammed my fist into its head, spinning it off me, then it collapsed onto the ground.

Something growled and hissed in the canopy. The second demon I'd just knocked to the floor hissed in response and ran away.

Winston ran after them, grunting as he went.

"We have to go," Ursula screamed and ran towards me. "The security guards are coming, and I overheard them phoning the police." She pulled on my elbow.

We ran. I jumped beside her in her car because I'd told Keith, the driver, to go back to the house, I didn't want him part of this.

Flashlights darted out of the darkness, trying to find the cause of the ruckus.

Ursula slammed her car in gear and sped away, spinning the wheels of her Ford Fiesta before finally pulling away in second gear. She smashed the gas as we went over a red light, something flashed in my face, blinding me.

"Shit, you're paying for that speeding ticket," Ursula said as she nervously glanced in the rear-view mirror. "Fuck, that was intense. Are you okay?" she asked, pulling my coat open to assess the damage.

"I'm fine," I shoved her hand away even though I winced. "Don't go back to the house. I have a suspicion they know where it is." I winced again when I tried to move. "Can we go somewhere for a while?"

"Yeah, sure."

"And slow down. You don't want the cops on your ass either."

Ursula nodded, eased off the gas and focused her attention on driving under the speed limit.

I leaned against the chairback and exhaled. Not like I needed to breathe, but it eased the pain in my abdomen. I hated those vile creatures, anything they touched needed careful cleaning. And I had two of those things inside me.

Chapter Ten

URSULA

I parked in my garage and closed the door. Declan flinched the moment the car stopped.

"Where are we?" he asked, sounding delirious.

"My house, let's go inside and see what's going on with that," I said, pointing at the blood stained wound.

I observed him as he struggled to grasp the car handle to open the door. His fingers reached out for it but missed it each time. He looked drunk. For a vampire, that was impossible. I grabbed his hand and steered it towards the handle and helped pull the car door open. He pushed open the door with his knee, turned his body and kicked it open all the way. Then he stumbled out, landing with a loud thud on the floor, knees first. He groaned, unmoving.

I watched how those demons dug into him, but he was a master vampire; he usually healed quickly.

"What did they do to you?" I asked as I slung my bag over my shoulder, slammed my door shut and ran around the car.

I gripped him under his arms and helped him to his

feet. He was fucking heavy, but he helped me to help him stand.

He slurred something I couldn't decipher.

"Just shut up and concentrate on walking. You weigh a ton. How the devil can a vampire weigh so much? It's like you're made of stone," I groaned as we headed for the kitchen door.

Once we were inside the house, I carefully sat him on the couch. I lifted his legs, but he just fell over with a loud thump.

"Declan?" I yelled, slapping his cheek. "Can you hear me? Do you need anything?"

Declan was unresponsive.

Ice filled my veins.

"No! Wake up!" I wanted to slap him again but couldn't hurt him. Instead, I pulled off his shirt and saw his marked body, the large gaping wounds gushing blood. If I didn't do something quickly, I wondered if he'd die. I didn't know the answer, but this was serious. There was too much blood and too many wounds. The demons had meant to kill him—and they almost succeeded.

All I thought about was saving him. I couldn't lose my Declan when I only just found him. I had to do everything to help him. If I stopped the bleeding, maybe he'd heal himself.

My heart raced at the thought of losing him. He was my savior and supposed to turn me into a vampire so I could work with him; spend the rest of my life with him.

I glanced down at his lifeless body; his skin already grey. I didn't know what to do except one thing; I'd have to treat him like a human and see if that worked. That's all I knew.

"I need the first aid kit," I mumbled to myself.

I dropped my bag and sprinted to the bathroom for a

towel and the large kit Mom had put together. Everything a surgeon needed for a basic procedure. I carried the heavy bag, dropped it to the floor and ran to the kitchen for a bowl and a bottle of water.

I opened the kit, pulled out solutions to clean the wounds, tweezers, gauze, and got to work cleaning him.

Vampires healed themselves from almost everything; but one swipe across their necks and their heads popping off would definitely kill them. If one pushed them out into the sun and they burned like a star, then they'd return to the earth as dust. But stab wounds, gunshots, and even limb amputation healed, making them whole again.

But Declan was centuries old, he should've healed. But he wasn't. I'd cleaned two of the wounds and his skin wasn't knitting together. There was nothing I could do...

Blood.

He needed blood to heal. Blood replenished them and he needed mine. It's not like we had a vending machine with blood packs, and it was too late for me to rush to a hospital. And I couldn't risk leaving him alone. I wasn't sure it would work, but right now that's all I had.

When I'd finished cleaning and bandaging him, I pressed my wrist to his mouth. Nothing.

"Stupid, he needs me to do it," I mumbled to myself, which seemed to happen often.

I grabbed the scalpel from the kit, sliced my wrist and pressed it to his open mouth. The moment my warm blood hit his lips; his eyes shot open, glowing crimson.

He turned his head towards me with a predatory gleam in his eye, a gasp escaping my lips. Declan forcefully gripped my hand and sucked on the wound. His eyes closed, and all I heard was my heart beating in my ears, Declan slurping my blood, and then feeling woozy.

Chapter Eleven

DECLAN

Her blood was heaven sent. Her divine life juice tasted like no other. This girl was... The sweetest. The purest. And the most delicious I'd ever had the pleasure of tasting. Oh, my gods...

I felt my wounds heal the moment her blood touched my lips and tongue. I felt her heat pour through me and down my throat as it worked through my veins; revitalizing me.

What was she? Her blood was not like any human I'd tasted before.

My eyes flitted open, and I cast my sights on her. She glowed golden. An aura of light surrounded her body. I gripped her hand and feasted on her delicious ichor. I drank her down until all the wounds had healed.

Ursula stared drunkenly at me and fell to the floor with me clutching her hand.

I knew I had to stop drinking from her golden well or I'd kill her, and she needed saving.

I unlatched my fangs from her delicate hand, kissed the

wound until it healed, and slowly sat up. My eyes darted around the busy room. On the walls hung portraits. Trinkets filled shelves. A bookshelf lined floor to ceiling with books on one side of the room, and mounds of stuff on the floor. On the opposite wall was a large cork board.

I flew up in one swift motion, forgetting about the numb-blood-drunk girl on the floor. The cork board took up the entire wall. One side had a map of the world with various pins stuck in with Post-it notes. One area I knew very well, and there was only one pin there. And in the middle of the board were notes of her spewing her thoughts along with pieces of wool connecting some notes to various pins on the map. Filled on the other side of the board, she'd stuck pictures of me; close ups, from a distance, some in black and white.

She's obsessed… with me.

A heated rage filled me as I tried to comprehend how the hell she got the pictures. We had conducted some of these meetings in secrecy; which no other had access to. Yet this little devil did and snapped shots of me.

I felt violated and chuckled at the irony of being stalked. I turned around to yell at her, but I couldn't. She lay on her side, the arm I'd bloodied now over her head when I dropped her.

An overwhelming need came over me, and I couldn't be mad at her. But I needed to know how she came about the information.

I stared at this human creature, my bite no doubt numbing her and blood loss too great for her to remain conscious.

Gently, I slipped my right hand under her legs, my left hand under her body, and set her gently on her couch. Grabbing the blanket from the edge of the couch, I placed it over her to keep her warm. She murmured something unintelligible as she fought her dreams. I pressed my hand to her forehead, and she settled down.

I wanted to understand what she was and sat beside her. The feeling of her blood tingled inside my mouth and throughout my body, alive with possibilities. I just didn't know what. And somehow, from ingesting her blood, I saw her surrounding glow.

I moved loose curls from Ursula's face, her skin as smooth as the most expensive porcelain doll ever made. Her red hair brightened into an intense shine, reminding me of the sun. Her body radiated warmth I'd forgotten; warmth of dawn, warmth on lazy summer days. Warmth I'd tried to forget yet would never.

Somewhere in the house I heard a beat. I placed my hand on Ursula's chest and felt her heartbeat steadily against my hand in time with the beat in the house. When I placed my hand over the part where my heart had stopped centuries ago—and felt it beat in time with hers.

Red tears splashed against her blanket. A hurricane of emotions smashed into me at once. This little minx had not only healed my wounds with speed, but she'd jump started my dark heart. The rhythm of mine connected with hers.

"Who are you?" I whispered into the air, hoping for an answer.

She started, slowly waking. "You're okay?" Ursula said groggily. She sat up, fought a dizzy spell, and leaned against the couch. "Your wounds… are they better now? How do you feel?"

"Take it easy, sunshine. Not so many questions until you can keep your eyes open," I said, smiling fondly. I stood, adding. "I feel fine. But more importantly, what are you?"

"Huh?" she asked as she swung her legs off the couch,

the numbing effect seeping away quicker than I'd ever seen. At least I knew of one human who wouldn't stay down for long after I'd bitten her.

Ursula kept the blanket close to her body and shivered. Her aura dimmed as she slowly noticed her surroundings. After her yawn and stretch her aura had almost disappeared.

"What are you?" I turned to her again, and she paled.

"Are you upset? Is it because I removed your shirt?"

"No," I came before her on one knee, my hands grasping hers. "What you are, Ursula?" Perhaps if I emphasized her name, she would tell me. "You offered me your blood, did you not?" She nodded carefully. "There is something in your blood I need to understand, because it's nothing I've ever tasted before. Again, I ask, what are you?"

Slowly her cheeks reddened, and she smiled. "I'm just a human, Declan. I'm serious. There's nothing magical or special about me. I'm a boring human."

I didn't believe her. There had to be a reason she wasn't telling me.

Her eyes flitted to the corkboard behind me, and her cheeks glowed a darker red. "You saw?" she asked and started biting her thumbnail.

"Yes, I saw your nasty obsession. You should be in a room with padded walls. It's unhealthy. No wonder you just about jumped my bones. The moment you saw an opening to kiss me, you stole it. I feel violated, Ursula. You should feel bad about yourself," I grinned. "Is that all I am to you? Just a body to use?" I teased.

She giggled nervously. "No, of course not."

I stood and glanced at the corkboard again. "Seriously though, do I have to worry? Are you going to kill me in my sleep?"

She burst out laughing. "No," she said, covering her mouth with her hand. "But yes, I was obsessed, not crazy obsessive, just madly in lo... Lust. But not anymore." She corrected herself and stood quickly, the blanket falling to the floor as she tried to step over it and away from me.

Did she think I wouldn't catch her slip?

"You said you didn't want me anymore after you kissed me." I stepped towards her. "You even gave Winston a look." I closed the gap.

She stared at me like a rabbit caught in my trap.

I pushed her against the wall with my body, my arms on either side of her head. Her chest rose and fell. She pressed her head against the wall, lifting her chin and stared at me with hooded eyes. Her mouth parting.

I leaned into her. I wanted her to feel the hardness of my body. She whimpered when my mouth found her cheek. "Don't you want me anymore?"

"You want Lana," she breathed. "You don't look at me the way you stare at her. Besides, you never even wanted me. So it's fine. And yes, I kissed you because the moment presented itself. But you want Lana—"

"You're right." And she was. Ursula was available now, and as much as I wanted to touch her, I wanted Lana more. I needed to stop giving in to temptation if I truly wanted Lana. I nodded and pushed away from the wall. "I do want Lana."

She smiled, cupped my face and kissed me chastely.

"Good boy. I'm sure you're a pretty good lay, but I'm not that into you as I thought I was." She shrugged nonchalantly. "Sorry."

Although she didn't say it, I was sure she liked Winston.

Chapter Twelve

DECLAN

Ursula gave Keith directions to her house so he could fetch me. Then I instructed Ursula to find out more about her bloodline. But when she'd told me her parents had died and there was no-one else, it left her stumped. And since she had no other relatives to ask, I told her to seek a witch. Witches —ancient and scary ones—could decipher her blood and advise on her origins. There were locations of supernaturals pinned to her corkboard where she could start.

While she did that, Keith and I headed back to the rental mansion.

It was past two in the morning when we got back. Winston was in his room, trying to trace where those demons had originated from.

Winston told me how he'd chased them over Table Mountain but when they split into different directions he struggled to keep up.

I sensed who had orchestrated this and needed to speak with the demon leader to stop these attacks. Otherwise, they'd just keep sending new demons after me. As I'd learned before, all demons had a price. I had to figure out what they wanted.

Oleg Larsen was your typical Norse man; sandy blond hair, bright blue eyes, and perfect features. But he was a cold killer, before he turned into a vampire. He was also the last human I'd turned—which I regretted. And I vowed never to turn anyone every again. Even though Ursula practically begged me, I wasn't sure whether I should. It was a decision I wouldn't take lightly ever again.

Oleg's number one goal was to be better than me in everything. And if I didn't accept the title and rule Krystal Creek, he would. He obviously wanted to remove the choice for me by having me killed while on vacation.

I'd already alerted the Council to the demon's actions, and that my stay was now compromised. I also informed them of my acceptance as Master Vampire for the town, which they welcomed. It would cut my stay here short since I now needed to take up residence, meet with the Master Vampire of Sterling Meadow, and bring more vampires into my kiss.

For now, half my worries were sorted. Next was finding out what Ursula was. Then destroy Oleg.

To help my thinking, I decided on an early morning dip in the ocean. I swam farther away from shore but stopped when splashing sounded behind me. I turned to find Lana swimming out to me. She was beautiful, even though she struggled to breathe through her waves.

She shouldn't be here.

"I distinctly remember telling you to stay away."

"I'm allowed to swim here too, you know," she grumbled affectionately.

"Are you stalking me, too?"

"Huh?" she said, brows knitting together as another

wave sprayed her in the face. She looked like a drowned rat, a very beautiful one I might add.

"I said, were you waiting for me to show up?" I smirked when she closed the gap.

"I couldn't sleep," she grinned.

"Oh, and why was that?"

"I was waiting for you," she said as she spat out salty water. "It worried me. You've been here every morning around three, but not today. I thought something happened. Then when something woke me, I took a chance and came out here. Then I saw you trying to swim like a seal." Her smile split her face in two.

I harrumphed. "I don't swim like a seal."

She laughed, making me laugh.

"And you just had to come say 'hi' at four in the morning?" I smirked.

She smiled sweetly. Her red-rimmed eyes translucent— no doubt an irritation from the salt water.

Based on Lana's actions my warning didn't work. She wanted me and I doubted nothing I said would stop her. And being the gentleman that I was, I would oblige.

"Understand, Lana, I've warned you to stay away. Are you prepared for what lies ahead?"

She nodded. "I understand."

"Are you sure? Because if we do this, there's no turning back?"

"I want this, Declan. I want you," she said seriously.

Silly girl. I doubted she understood what her actions really meant. What I would do to her... Her tempting me would end in satisfaction, at least. A broken heart I didn't care for. That's not what I did. But...

We swam closer to the shore but didn't swim out

completely. We waded in the water, moving over the waves in silence; she stared at me, and I was transfixed on her.

For the first time in my long life, I stared, speechless. Lana's beauty knocked the words right out of me. But something else gnawed at me. My conflicting argument with myself as I gravitated slightly towards Ursula and the secrets she held. Ursula made it clear what she thought of me, and it relieved me. I wouldn't be breaking her heart soon—if ever. But drinking her blood had bonded us in some way, yet to be discovered.

Then there was Lana, who stared at me with purity and innocence I couldn't ignore. There was something about her that pulled me in deeply and wholly. Her sandy brown hair darkened when wet. Her beautiful smile and sparkling green eyes brightened her face. Then there was her calm demeanor setting me at ease.

There was only one thing left to do.

I navigated closer to her. My eyes raked down the parts of her body I could see before the deeper waters covered her. The sight of her naked breasts and hard buds made me hard, aching to touch every inch of her.

Closing the gap, I wrapped my arms around her warm, naked body and pulled her against me. Time stood still as we conveyed our feelings through unspoken words that only pulled us closer.

My eyes flitted down to her nose and then her plump red lips; lips I needed to taste. With our faces inches apart, I didn't hesitate; I bruised her mouth as Lana clung to my shoulders. She didn't stop me or push me away, instead she opened her mouth for my tongue. She tasted sweet and a little minty. I smiled in the kiss; she prepared for this kiss. She wanted other things when she wrapped her legs around my waist with my hardness pressed against her delicate skin. I groaned as she rocked against me.

When I pulled away, there was an unmistakable hunger in her eyes. A hunger I aimed to satisfy. I let go of her and reluctantly unhooked her legs from me. She pouted. Little did she know I wasn't done, not yet, and grabbed her hand. As we neared the shore, our feet touched the sand and seaweed hugged our ankles. But before we walked all the way out, I stopped.

She stared up at me, waiting, wanting. Her eyes greedy for my lips as she licked salt from her own. She let go of my hand and held my waist as she nestled under my arm. My body stiffened with her warm body near mine, and I needed to taste her. I needed to know how she felt beneath me, and how she felt inside. I wanted my hands to caress her skin, to feel every part of her.

I wanted her.

But Lana was the type who wanted her man all to herself. While I'd never considered only having one woman at a time; I'd had many and many at once. I'd been a bachelor for centuries, no one woman had ever caught my eye where I only wanted her alone. Yet, as I stared down at this beauty holding on to me, I shuddered thinking what I'd do if I lost her. She wouldn't want to share me, and I didn't want to share her either. Something tugged somewhere inside that hollow cavity where my heart had somehow thudded when I was with Ursula. But this time it was a different clunk, like cog wheels turning, and my chest squeezed ever so slightly as something within me bloomed.

My feelings and thoughts were foreign, leaving me unsure and slightly queasy. I needed to think hard about whatever was going on. But for now, this moment we shared, I'd give Lana every part of me.

My right hand snaked through her hair and the other kept her hips close to my body. I licked her lips, teasing the slit so delicately. She closed her eyes and parted her mouth. I plunged my tongue into her warm opening to taste, to lick, to tease. Her tongue danced with mine as she moaned.

She couldn't get enough, but neither could I.

I walked us out of the water toward the clothing. Slowly she sat on her opened towel while I hovered above her, our lips never leaving. She opened her legs wider for me, her hand grabbed my ass bringing me closer. She laid down while I followed her, careful not to crush her with my body.

Her hand reached for my steel shaft and with a shaky hand gently stroked up and down. I moaned in the kiss as my left elbow rested beside her head while my right hand found her warm, slick folds. We played with each other, finding what made the other moan.

Feeling more assertive in her actions, she applied pressure as she moved her hand up and down, while I slipped a finger inside her heated sheath, then two. She let go of me when I pumped my fingers, drawing out mewling sounds from her opened mouth. I slowed the rhythm as her climax hit her, but maintained that delicious thrust while rubbing her ripe clit.

"I want you inside me," she said hoarsely, grabbing me once more and guided me towards her slick folds.

Not wanting to let the lady down, I eased inside. Her eyes glazed over as she clutched my shoulders, her fingernails digging into my skin. Lana winced as I pushed deeper, then visibly relaxed once I'd filled her completely. I wasn't all the way inside her heated sheath, but I felt I could go no farther. I eased back out as she coated me with her juices and slowly pushed back inside, taking it an inch at a time.

She moaned as I found my rhythm within her; she was

hot and incredibly tight, testing my control. All I wanted to do was fuck her hard and tear screams from her. But I didn't want to hurt her, and I wanted to enjoy every moment with her.

Then with slow even strokes, I continued easing myself in and out of her gently, not too hard, and didn't push too deep.

She tilted her hips, meeting each of my thrusts, wanting more. I increased my speed and pushed a little deeper with each powerful thrust.

I groaned when Lana breathed in panted gasps. Then after that it didn't take long; her body tensed around me, and she dug her nails into my back, reveling in the sensations.

When she relaxed, I had space to thrust deeper and harder. When she clenched her stomach muscles once more and called my name, my balls tightened. Lana grabbed my ass, driving me mad, and I sought release within her.

Lana's body trembled beneath me as I slowly eased out of her and laid beside her.

Chapter Thirteen

LANA

Oh my gods, oh my gods, oh my gods. That was the best experience ever! I couldn't believe I just did that. I felt my cheeks heat, my heart raced, and I couldn't stop smiling.

"What's going on in your head?" Declan asked and kissed my temple. I felt his gaze on my body and all the hair on my body stood on end.

"That was amazing," I said, followed by a giggle.

"You're bleeding," Declan said through a low growl and reached for me. "Did I hurt you?" he asked, sounding panicked.

"No, ah." I sat quickly, grabbed my shirt and slipped it on, then my pants. "It's nothing."

"Were you a virgin?" he asked with compassion and what sounded like shock.

"Uh," I shrugged.

"Christ." He stood, pinching the bridge of his nose, and shook his head.

My heart sank, and tears welled in my eyes. My breath hitched as I picked up my towel and shook out the sand.

That wasn't the reaction I wanted. I didn't want him to know.

"How old are you?"

"What does it matter? It just never happened okay." Tears fell as I continued shaking out my towel, folded it roughly, and tucked it under my arm. "You didn't have to react like that."

"No, honey," he said gently, grabbing my shoulders to stop me from storming off. "That's not what I meant. Just," — he kissed my temple, — "if I'd known I would've been gentler." He pulled me into the curve of his body.

The moment his arms wrapped around me, I cried. All the pent-up anxiety of it all, then finally doing it over-whelmed me.

"Hey," he said as he consoled me. "It's okay." He pressed his lips to my forehead, and I felt him shake his head. "I just wish I'd known, then I would've made it special, not out here in the cold with sand getting every-where." He dusted sand off my back.

I burst out laughing. "You're cheesy, do you know that? I didn't want that. This was perfect. It was everything I wanted, it really was," I said, nodding and dusted the tears from my face.

Declan cupped my face and wiped the last tear with his thumb and then over my bottom lip. His intense blue eyes stared hungrily, but kindly. He kissed me one last time, lingering before letting go.

"Are you hurt?"

I shook my head a little too enthusiastically. "No, I'm fine." I really was. It wasn't sore at all, he was big, but it didn't hurt. He made it enjoyable, and boy was it the most pleasur-able experience of my life. I felt my entire neck and face heat.

He smiled knowingly, his eyes hinting that it's possible he knew what I was thinking. "Let me walk you home—"

"No, I can manage."

"No!" He ordered. "Allow me to ensure your safety."

Declan dressed quickly, his damp clothing highlighting his honed body and each curve of his muscles. I tried hard not to touch him. He slipped his hand in mine and held me close. I leaned my head against his shoulder as we walked the path to my home. We stopped near my entrance; I opened the gate, and he continued following me up the stairs. I opened the door to my small apartment above the garage.

"Is this where you live?"

"Yeah, when my dad remarried, she really didn't want me in the house with them. She said I was old enough to live on my own. But my dad wanted me nearby. So, this was the compromise she made."

Declan shook his head. "How often do you see your dad?"

"About once a month. They keep to themselves, but they travel a lot. She's loaded and well, they keep each other company I suppose. They're at that age where they've both retired and enjoying their lives."

"Where is your mom?"

"She died—"

"I'm sorry."

"It's okay. It happens."

We stared at each other for a heartbeat. I'd love for him to stay the night, to cuddle and whisper sweet nothings to each other until the sun splashed its warmth across our naked bodies, but I doubted it would happen. He seemed more the type who asked the girl to leave with her clothing tucked under her arms and had his butler escort her out—and he never fucked her twice.

At least now that I did it, I'd finally had sex, I didn't have to feel so apprehensive about it. There were at least five encounters where something could've happened, but we were interrupted, and it never happened.

Unfortunately, I never had a boyfriend longer than a week; most likely due to my reluctance to sleep with them on the first date. I was content with kissing and touching while they always wanted more too soon.

"How old are you?"

"Twenty-two." I wasn't that old; I'd heard of some girls losing their virginity when they were like twenty-eight.

"Huh," he said as he lifted his chin, no doubt thinking about something.

The air felt thick and uncomfortable. I yawned. I was getting tired and needed to get up at twelve for my shift in the afternoon since I only worked half days, but it was fine for now. I'd look for something more permanent once I found my feet. Then I'd rent a place of my own, get a full-time job and find someone who wanted to stick around longer than a week.

I stared at Declan and wondered whether he was the type, then shook the thought away. He was an American and would go home soon. This was only a onetime thing, and I expected nothing of him, although I wouldn't mind doing it again. There was nothing wrong with making sure the second time around was as enjoyable as the first. I grinned inwardly.

I yawned again, trying to nudge him away before we suffocated on the awkwardness of our current situation.

"I'd like to sleep now." I finally said, trying not to sound too awful about asking him to leave.

"Oh yes, of course." He leaned in and kissed my cheek. "I'll see you around then?" he asked cautiously, then headed for the door and opened it. "I really wish you'd told me, Lana, I would've done a lot of things differently."

"It's okay, Declan, really. It's how I wanted it. With you not knowing, I didn't feel so uncomfortable. It was perfect."

He nodded curtly, closing the door quietly behind him.

Chapter Fourteen

URSULA

I watched Keith pull up to my house with Winston in the passenger seat. I felt my forehead crinkle as I mouthed why he was with.

"I know you heard me," I said when I opened the car door.

"I did," Winston smiled, and it reached his sparkling green eyes. He pulled the visor down, staring at me through the little mirror. "Declan instructed I drive with Keith to take you where you need to go."

"I'm sure you were up all night...." I glanced nervously at Keith, who focused on the road. I doubted they told him who they really were and what they were doing. And I wasn't going to be the one to share their secret either.

"I need little sleep," Winston winked wickedly, forcing me to smile.

There was something about Winston that made me glance in his direction and every time I did, he was already staring at me. Typically, his action would've sent me into the fight or flight mode, yet his playful demeanor kept me engaged. I'd smile, then he'd smile.

"Where are we going?" Keith asked, bringing us out of our staring contest. We stopped at the red light.

"Go left at the robot." I pointed at the road Keith had to take.

I felt Winston's gaze on me; I glanced up to see his frown.

"What?"

"Robot?"

"Yeah, those three lights over there—"

"Traffic light."

"Yes, that."

Winston shook his head. "South Africans are confusing. To us, a robot is a little mechanical machine that mimics human movements because it's programmed that way."

"Well, we programmed the lights."

He snorted.

When I glanced at him again, his green eyes glowed yellow/brown, making me flinch. He winked again, as if doing that relaxed me. I knew he wouldn't eat me. But I didn't relax completely either. He was a wolf and enjoyed flesh, and I had a lot of it. There was enough meat and fat on my bones to satisfy any supernatural creature. Although I felt comfortable around Winston, I would never let my guard down while I was still human. Perhaps I'd relax once Declan turned me into a vampire.

When I found the piece of paper I'd scribbled the address on, I handed it to Keith. He entered the details into the navigator system, activating her. We listened to her soothing voice guide us along the way.

We travelled north along the R27 towards Yzterfontein,

otherwise known as Iron Fountain. I enjoyed expansive views of the blue ocean on our left with undisturbed fynbos on our right. We'd been on the road for an hour when we finally arrived at the hidden gem. We continued through the tiny town until we made our way to the very last house at the end of the road.

I'd only been to Yzterfontein once before, on holiday with my parents before they died. This was why this place existed; purely for holidays. The town was quiet, with only a nine kilometer stretch of road through the entire place with quirky stops for refreshments or to take in the sights.

The blue bay was cold because of the Benguela current, but that didn't stop surfers or swimmers from bracing the icy waters. Those wanting to escape the city life frequented the resorts or owners came to spend a weekend at their second home.

I remembered walking the twenty-five-kilometer beach trail in the early morning with my parents, and we watched the sun rise as we plodded along the beach. The salty water sprayed against our faces and body while the wind blew it dry.

My chest tightened at the thought of my parents, and then the loss soon thereafter. My mother was dying of cancer, but she braved the hike. And my dad had loved my mother so much he couldn't bear to live without her for long and died in his sleep a month after her passing. Those two months were the worst, two funerals, two burials, and forever alone; a thirty-something year old orphan.

Keith parked the vehicle in the driveway of one of the oldest houses in the street. It literally stood at the end of the road with a white picket fence surrounding the white wooden house. I noted brown sections on the weathered building, realizing nothing stayed beautiful all year round.

"Winston, can you come with?" I asked as I opened the car door.

"Are you sure?"

I nodded and climbed out of the car.

Winston followed close behind me. I glanced over my shoulder and his green eyes held warmth and kindness. To me, he seemed like an old soul with a dark streak. He also took care of others before himself. But, if you messed with him, he'd bite your hand off or go straight for your jugular for that pulsing vein.

Winston may be a bit on the short side, but I was sure he made up for it in other areas. My cheeks glowed at the naughty thought and smiled at him, then braced myself for what lay just beyond the door.

After I'd given Declan my blood and I was no longer dizzy, he had explained how it made him feel. I honestly didn't believe it, there was no way my blood could do what he'd described. And the fact he'd seen my aura as golden was surreal. But then again, he was the first immortal to have tasted my blood. There was no way of me knowing any different. I'd never donated blood and the more I thought about it, I'd never visited the doctor either. My mother had always said she was lucky, I was a healthy kid.

I sucked in air and knocked. Before I could ring the doorbell, the door opened.

Amahle glanced at me with deep brown eyes and an enormous smile. "You're just in time, my dear," she said and opened the door wider, her Venda bracelets jingling. She opened her other arm wider, her threadbare dress clinging to her slim body with more makunda bracelets on her other wrist. "Please come in. And who is the guest?" she asked when she saw Winston. She sniffed the air and smiled knowingly, then cast a suspicious eye at me.

"A friend. If that's okay?"

"Yes, it is your choice. Come in. Come in."

I entered her living room. Adorned on the walls were shelves filled with various jars that would make anyone afraid. After my parents' deaths, I did a lot of soul searching and read up on every supernatural I got my hands on. I couldn't explain why, but I always had an inclination towards that side. I already knew about vampires and were-wolves, so I studied our witch doctors or sangoma's and inyanda's.

Inyanda's were usually male and herbalists, while a sangoma was a diviner and usually female. She would operate within a traditional religious supernatural context and acted as a medium between the mortal world and ancestral spirits. A sangoma's job was to diagnose unexplainable illnesses by interpreting messages from the ancestors, while prescribing medicine for identifiable conditions.

And that's why I was here. I needed Amahle to see what I was by asking my ancestors. I didn't know of relatives to ask, and she was my link to the other side.

"Sit." Amahle pointed to the carpet on the floor.

I followed her lead and sat down. Winston sat beside me, but a little back. I grabbed his knee for moral support and squeezed. My heart raced in my chest, and I didn't know why. There was nothing for me to be afraid of unless it was just nerves.

I glanced up at the jars on the shelves, most likely divided into the various powders for bathing, ingesting, or rubbing on the skin or wounds. I wondered if I had to use any of them. The smell of spices and saw dust filled my nostrils, and I stifled a sneeze.

Amahle cleared her throat. Her lips curved at the sides, brightening her face.

"Don't be nervous, child." She reached for my hand and patted it. "It's going to be alright. You've come to the right place."

I reached for my purse to pay, but she shook her head. "After."

"Okay."

Amahle placed her hands on her knees, palms side up, her legs crossed beneath her, her back straight and eyes closed. She hummed. A spike of something shot through the air and my arms pebbled. I glanced over at Winston, who stared wide eyed and shrugged.

Amahle grunted, moving her body in a tight circle while keeping her hands on her knees. She stilled and opened her eyes, reached behind her and lit something.

"I'm going to burn the imphepho plant. It helps me summon the ancestors." She hummed, then nodded. "I'm rather curious as to your reason you came to me, a black sangoma. Usually those seeking white ancestors went elsewhere."

"Yes, well..." I glanced nervously at Winston again. "My mother was... of color. She married a German man while studying abroad."

"Ah, that explains why I see your aura the way I do. Do you know you have light within you?"

I shrugged. "I don't know what that means."

Amahle's eyes flitted to Winston, then back to me. "He knows, don't you?"

Winston nodded. "When I look at her, I sense something but not sure what."

Amahle smiled but didn't offer any information.

"Well, would someone please tell me?"

"You are a natural healer, child. Your aura doesn't merely shine, it glows," she grinned. "You are beautiful."

She pressed a button on her remote and drumming started, echoing in the small room. "I see those who they truly are," she nodded at Winston. "He's a protector; not only for you but for a man. A powerful being who will be coming into much, much, more power than he had ever thought." She started convulsing as the drumming became louder and more erratic. I wanted to jump up and help her, but Winston grabbed my upper arm and shook his head. This was what she did. This was how she communicated with the *others*, with the ancestors. I could only hope she spoke to mine.

After five minutes, the drumming lulled into a softer, gentler rhythm. Amahle stopped convulsing and started humming again. She reached behind her back and produced a bag. She shook it and spilled the contents on the carpet before me; a random collection of twigs, bones, shells, semi-precious stones, hair, and coins. She hovered her hands above the items, mumbling words I couldn't decipher. Her eyes rolled into the back of her head, the air snapped, heat caressed my face, and something slapped my arm, followed by liquid dripping down to my elbow. When I wiped my arm, my hand came away with blood.

"I don't know what did it but they," — Winston pointed into the air, — "needed your blood."

Amahle stuck her tongue out, something red smeared on her tongue, and she tasted it. She opened her eyes, the black orbs piercing my soul. My heart stuttered, then raced. My skin broke out in a layer of sweat and my tongue thick with no words.

"They have spoken to me, Ursula," Amahle breathed as if her lungs constricted. She closed her eyes once more, when she opened them again, they were her usual hazel color. "Uh, I see why. I understand. Yes," she nodded, mumbling to herself, not quite making sense. "You are a Child of the Sun, and you possess remarkable healing capabilities. You need to be treasured—"

"I don't understand. What does it mean?"

"Children of the Sun are rare. Once revealed, others sacrifice them." Her eyes fluttered as if possessed. She gained her strength and continued speaking. "They are usually very fare skinned, with white hair and eyebrows. Not only are you a Child of the Sun, but a potent healer. My child, nobody," she whispered. "Nobody," she repeated in a low tone, making me shiver, "should know who you are and what you can do. If they do, your life is in grave danger." She choked on her words.

For a moment there was silence and I stopped breathing waiting in anticipation.

"Oh, no!" She shook her head. "It's too late. They have heard the words I've spoken. They will come. You," she pointed at Winston, "need to take her out of the country. They cannot find her. Do you understand? If they do…" She stared at me for a moment too long, making my heart thunder in my chest. "They will slaughter her." She stood, motioning for us to get up and shooed us out. When I offered her payment, she shook her head. "No, I've done enough damage. By calling on your ancestors, I've alerted others to you. I'm sorry, dear. I should have known." A tear slipped down her cheek. "They will come for you, my child. Stay hidden. Stay safe."

Relief washed over me once we were back in the car, heading to Cape Town. I sat in the backseat, practically on

Winston's lap. He draped an arm around me and held my hand.

My body trembled as I thought about Amahle's words, and I didn't want to be alone. I didn't want space. I needed closeness, and Winston was the closest to me.

Sweat dripped down my back and beaded my forehead even though the air-con blasted cold air. I shimmied closer to Winston, if that was at all possible. He pulled me into the curve of his powerful body and his heat warmed me.

Winston leaned closer and spoke near my ear, making my arms pebble. "I will inform Declan about what had happened. And I think you should pack a bag from your house and stay with us until we can ensure your safety."

"And then what?" I glanced up at him, our faces only centimeters apart, his warm breath against my cheek. "I knew there's a reason I wanted to leave with you—with Declan."

He shrugged. "I will try, okay?"

I smiled nervously and snuggled into his comforting body.

Ever since I dug deeper into the supernatural world and had come across Declan, I knew there was a reason I gravitated towards him. Almost instinctively, I had to do every-thing—*everything*—in my power to get near him. This was why.

Yes, I was deeply obsessed with him. I wanted him. My infatuation with him was more than just what I thought. He was my salvation. He would be the one to keep me from harm. And even though I kissed him, my crush had fizzled out instantaneously, my itch scratched. I enjoyed it, I really did, but it lacked something. He wasn't lacking, but some-thing between us was.

Did I like Declan? Yes.

Did I want to be with him? No, I wanted to work with him. I wanted to be part of his kiss if he'd just turn me.

This was what I was meant to do. And from what the sangoma had said, I was on the right track.

I shuddered at what the alternative might be... *death*.

Chapter Fifteen

DECLAN

I paced the lounge while the girl fluttered around me like a butterfly. The maid, Nancy, kept cleaning after me. Finally, I shoved her out of my way and told her to leave. She cried as she ran downstairs to her accommodation. I felt like a dick. But there was stuff happening, and I couldn't have her scurrying around me.

"Was that necessary, Master?" Winston asked as he dipped low.

I arched an eyebrow and glanced at the shattered glass on the floor, the broken plates and the coffee maker broken in the corner. "Of course it's necessary. I'm angry."

"Well, this won't make it better—"

I growled at him, baring my emerging fangs, and my eyes glowed red like they always did when I was angry.

Winston raised his hands in submission. "I'm merely pointing out that you didn't have to yell at the poor girl. She was cleaning your mess."

"Thank you, Watson, tell me something I don't know."

It was his turn to growl at the sound of my pet name for him.

"Enough!" Ursula yelled, placing a calming hand on my chest. "It's enough," she whispered. "You've told your people you're taking the job. Now turn me and let's leave."

I shook my head and removed her wrist from me before I broke it. "Don't touch me like that again. I don't care how unique and delicious your blood is, I will drain you if you touch me again. I'm not some child you're trying to calm down."

"Then stop acting like one," she said sternly. "You need to fight the demons, not us. Do you want the South African police knocking on this door? Then carry on." She leaned back against the kitchen island with her arms crossed over her chest, making her cleavage prominent. "And stop staring at my breasts," she moaned and dropped her arms to her sides.

The demon leader had reached out first and asked to meet with me. They agreed not to attack us, only to discuss a very delicate subject. I stared at the subject—*Ursula*. The person she had sought for guidance had awoken the entire fucking supernatural world. They all knew what she was now. Even the Vampire Council said that if I came across her, I should acquire her.

Not only was she a fantastic kisser, a healer, but a Child of the Sun. Which meant every bastard wanted her. They'd most likely cage her and take as much of her blood as they could without killing her; every single day until she was old or worse, when they finally killed her.

To deter others, I could turn her into a night hunter and have her join my kiss. The risk of contaminating her blood was great, but it would save her life.

She stared at me with pleading eyes.

"You've caused a clusterfuck you know."

"You told me to ask, dickhead." She slapped my shoulder. "Don't blame this on me." The lines between her brows deepened, and she huffed.

Winston coughed into his hand, his eyes flitting from me then to Ursula, waiting for me to rip her head off.

Nobody spoke to me that way. But I couldn't be angry with her. It was my fault she was in this mess. Dammit, I couldn't be angry. I burst out laughing. The air seemed to lighten as the tension between my shoulders eased.

"Fuck." I shook my head, rubbing my face with both hands. My fangs elongating as I smelled a familiar scent that made me stiffen. A soft knock on the glass door from outside caught my attention, and I hissed.

"Hi," Lana said carefully as she entered. "I thought I'd pop in quickly."

"I really wish you'd call first, we're actually on our way out." I struggled to keep the irritation out of my voice. I didn't mean for it, but she was the recipient all the same.

She stopped near the door and her expression dropped along with her shoulders. She blinked back tears. "I just wanted to let you know you wouldn't see me tonight… uh, you know." She shrugged uncertainly. Her eyes flicked from me to Winston, then Ursula. "Sorry," she mumbled, darting out the door and ran down the steps.

"Christ!" I really didn't need her guilt on me today either.

"Go after her, Declan, and stop being a dick. You just hurt her feelings," Ursula said as she pushed me. "She's young and has lots to learn, but you didn't have to speak to her that way." She pushed me again.

"Okay, just stop shoving me." I side-eyed Winston, who nodded; our silent conversation understood—he would set up the meeting with the demons. Now all we needed was to get this party started.

Chapter Sixteen

LANA

I felt pathetic. A young girl who got upset for the smallest things. Was it because he was my first that whatever he said affected me more than it should? Others had spoken to me like that before, but when Declan spoke that way it... hurt... bruised... left me confused.

My head ached from the pounding migraine blooming inside my head. Sometimes it happened when I cried; as if the force of trying not to cry was greater than when I did eventually cry. The flood gates burst, leaving me with a crater to fix with pain medication.

I felt pathetic.

I stomped away from a man I barely knew and had only slept with once. He spoke to me with irritation laced in his words and probably not meant for me, but I took them personally.

"Lana!" Declan called behind me, his footsteps quickening.

I continued stomping without glancing over my shoulder.

"Wait, will you?" He grabbed my arm, but I yanked it out of his grasp. "Please, wait. I'm sorry I was a dick back there."

I stopped and scowled up at him.

He gripped the top of my arms firmly without hurting me. I suspected he was trying to keep me there and not run away again. He glanced around to see if anyone was watching, then cupped my face. His hands were cold against my warm skin and sent a shiver down my spine. His warm lips touched mine and I should've pushed him away, but I didn't. I kept my arms crossed though, keeping him away from my body.

"I'm sorry. It's not aimed at you. There's shit going on and I don't want you involved. Please accept my apology."

I blinked back the flood gates but kept staring at his deep blue eyes that held humor.

"Now tell me, why won't I see you tonight?" He smirked, looking as handsome as ever, and I hated him for it. I pushed away from him. "No, don't do that." He grabbed me, pulling me into an embrace.

I relented and wrapped my arms around him, pressing my head against his chest, and frowned. "I can barely hear your heartbeat." He stiffened.

"Where are you going?" He asked carefully, placing his chin on the top of my head.

I exhaled a shaky breath. "I'm going out with a few friends tonight—"

"Hey, Lana, hurry will you," Denis yelled, waving me over. They were waiting for me in the parking area.

"Who is he?" Declan growled; I felt a low rumbling in his chest.

"Are you jealous?" I teased, creating distance between us and glanced up at him.

Declan's expression frightened me; his eyes seemed to pierce my body, carving me open and exposing my soul. I shuddered.

"I don't like him. He only wants one thing." Declan sniffed the air, tore his stare away from me and glowered at the car with my friends.

"I work with him. He's harmless. We're just going for a movie and drinks afterwards. I wanted to let you know I might not see you. It will depend on how late they drop me off."

"Who else are you going with?" He turned his dark gaze back on me.

"Denis, Mandy, and Estelle. We all work together in finance. Why should you care?"

I didn't know what we were or if we were even a thing. He was otherworldly with his bright crimson eyes when he yelled, pale skinned and blood lust. I expected nothing from him, but he drew me to him like an addict needing the next hit. He was American and leaving soon. I was just another notch in his belt, and I would gladly accept that role. My life was here, all I had to do was establish what I wanted.

Declan unclenched his fingers from my arms and stepped back. A whirl of conflicting emotions crossed his features, and I couldn't narrow any of them down. It confused me.

"You're right, I haven't claimed you as mine. I have no right over you." He sounded sad, defeated.

I wasn't expecting him to profess his love for me, but I didn't expect him to give up so easily. Perhaps it was for the best. It wouldn't have worked. And I should stop coming for my late evening, early morning swim until he left.

"Okay then," I said. "Fine!" My voice sounded small

and insignificant, like I wasn't sure or didn't really want to go with Denis.

I didn't walk away, and neither did Declan.

My heart raced as my indecisions smacked me against the side of my head. It would be good for me to go out with my friends. They were my age, did the things I liked—or so I thought since we hardly spent time together as a group outside of work.

But I wanted to stay with Declan; I sounded like a groupie.

"Do you want to go with them?"

Did I? If I thought hard about it, I didn't reeeally want to. I knew I had to make more friends, and this was a good starting point.

"Not really," I finally said as I glanced over my shoulder at the car. "But you said you had plans."

Declan cleared his throat. He seemed uncertain, then finally said, "I do, but would you like to stick around with me all the same?"

Something burst inside my chest; a box of happiness floated within me, and my heart stuttered. A smile flitted across my face, and I nodded.

"I would rather spend time with you."

He smiled. "Good, then tell your friends you'll take a raincheck and spend your evening with me."

Chapter Seventeen

DECLAN

What the actual hell was I doing? I should've just let Lana go with her human friends. She needed to be with them. But I couldn't. I stared into her emerald-green eyes, silently begging me to ask her to stay, and I couldn't let her go. I was crazy for liking this human girl, yet here I was—enjoying it way too much.

I'd have to tell her what I was and if she freaked out, I'd wipe her memory so she wouldn't remember anything about me and move on. The last thing I wanted was a freaked-out girl while we were on our way to a group of demons.

I should've asked Ursula if she thought Lana knew about my world. But it was too late now.

Lana scampered down the stairs towards me. I groaned inwardly. Even her actions were childlike, naïve, and so scrumptious I could eat her right here. I'd love to know what her blood tasted like—if she freaked out, I'd bite her, numb her, then manipulate her memory. I rarely performed mind compulsion, but I'd make an exception.

"It's fine." She slipped her arm through mine. "So, what are we doing?"

Chapter Eighteen

URSULA

I watched Winston give Declan a respectful glare that told me he did not approve of Lana joining us. Declan shrugged, not answering him.

We dropped the men at the rendezvous where they'd walk the short distance to Cape Point. They'd agreed to meet the demons there. When I'd asked Declan how he and Winston were going to get back to us, since Keith was driving us around, he grinned, whispered near my ear. "I can fly, dear." I thought he was joking, he wasn't. I didn't know about all his powers and guessed he could levitate.

We sat at a pizzeria near Simon's Town. From our seats we saw the dark ocean, the waves crashing against the shore only a short road crossing away.

The ambiance of the quaint pizzeria made one feel at home, with tantalizing smells of pizza, garlic, and cheese making me salivate.

Declan wanted us far away from the demons, but still close enough in case we needed them. Even though I didn't like it, I couldn't make him do anything he didn't want to do.

While they attended their meeting, Keith remained with us in case we needed to leave in a hurry.

Lana didn't know what was going on. As much as I wanted to tell her, it wasn't my secret to share. Whenever she asked what they were doing, I skirted along the truth and just said they had business to take care of.

Keith was a man of few words but did his jobs superbly. He kept the conversation going with Lana by asking her many questions about herself. My guess, he too suspected something amiss about the two men and wanted to help by distracting Lana with questions—which was sweet.

"How's your dad doing?" I asked Lana, then forked some of my steak. We'd known each other from surf school. She attended the lessons for kids while I the advanced sessions. After our lessons ended, I'd surf with her, or we'd swim in the sea together. Our parents had bonded while they watched us surf. Unfortunately, we drifted apart when we both suffered a loss the same year. Then when her dad remarried, and I needed to work, we hardly saw each other —until I saw her again when she entered Declan's rental home a couple of days ago.

"Oh, you know." She rolled her eyes.

"I never liked her."

"You and me both. Luckily, I hardly see her. They're in Hawaii until next week, then they're going to Barcelona."

"Jeez, I didn't know she was so loaded."

Lana nodded, slurping on her straw. "Anyway, just as long as I speak with my dad once a month, I'm happy. He's all I have left, but he needs to enjoy his life. If he's happy, I'm happy."

"Keith, block your ears, we're gonna chat about boys."

Keith groaned and shoveled the rest of his burger into his mouth. "Talk, I don't mind."

"So you and Declan…" I nudged. "I'd have never thought he was your type."

Her cheeks glowed.

"He's easy on the eyes and oozes deliciousness, revealing his bad boy side," I said, wiggling my eyebrows.

The Lana I remembered was a very good girl who rarely travelled on the wild side. Yet, Declan had his hooks in her and somehow, she had him around her little pinkie finger. He looked like a lost puppy when he brought her with. It was endearing, but unlike him from what I'd seen of him.

"It's strange, but there's something about him I can't stay away from. He isn't really my type, and like you say, he gives off that bad boy, scary vibe, but I like him," she grinned harder, and her eyes twinkled.

Lana was about ten years my junior, but she was one of the kindest souls I'd ever known. She didn't make you feel bad about swearing or drinking too fast. She might not want to partake in drinking games, but she still treated you with respect and kindness. I suspected because of her, Declan wanted to be a better man/vampire.

Keith's cellphone pinged. He read the message. His eyes widened, followed by swear words.

His swearing and the pinging of messages told me there was trouble. Something went wrong with their meeting, and we were in danger.

"We have to go, but not to the house. Somewhere else." He glanced at me as if waiting for me to give orders. I shrugged. He got another text message. "A hotel, any hotel. Come, grab your things let's go."

Lana protested, wanting to know what was going on, but Keith ignored us and headed for the exit.

We paid for our food and left, quickly climbed into the car and Keith drove like a bat out of hell.

Chapter Nineteen

DECLAN

"I don't like that you brought Lana, Master," Winston complained beside me. "Why did you bring her?" He asked as we slinked up the mountain to the New Cape Point Lighthouse. With no humans around, we moved freely up the path like a dark wind.

I didn't know how to answer his question because I couldn't bring myself to admit I liked the girl and didn't want anyone else near her.

When my silence wasn't good enough, he continued his ramblings. "If you like her, you need to tell her what she's in for. And you need to decide if she's coming with us. And Ursula. You can't keep either woman in the dark."

I stopped and glowered down at the little wolf-man.

"Master." He enunciated the word with such sarcasm all I could do was chuckle.

"I hate you, Watson. Do you know that?" I continued walking and sighed. "What do you think?"

"Me?"

"No, the wolf next to you. Of course, you."

"Well, I don't mind Ursula. She's in danger and she still wants you to bite her. Or I could bite her."

His confession stopped me mid-step, and I almost tumbled. "In all the years you never wanted to bite a female. Do you like her so much you would considered it?"

"Yes, but she wants to be a vampire."

"True. Okay, fine." I'd resigned to the idea. "I'll change her. Or we can give her the option. Just as long as it puts an end to this race to get her. If she's bitten, it might alter her blood and it will piss off the Council once they hear what we've done."

"They may accept it if she's a vampire. Maybe her blood remains pure, but the others will have no choice but to leave her alone. All the vampires will protect her, well, mostly all. She could even offer her blood to the Council as a thank you for acceptance."

"Her blood is so divine." A shiver ran through me. "It would be a shame if it changed."

I heard him sigh loudly but ignored him.

"If she's a wolf, you could still drink from her. And she'd have vampires and wolves as protection. We could join the wolves of Sterling Meadow and the smaller pack in Krystal Creek."

"You know, Watson, that's an awfully brilliant idea." I slapped his back. "We'll ask."

We stopped when we saw the row of glowing red eyes, their bodies blending with the dark skies and sea behind them. They stood on the cliff with the Lighthouse to one side and behind them.

One pair of eyes approached, and his body materialized; his coal-colored skin cracked as he moved, and each thinly sliced crevice breathed smoke with fine lines of moving lava beneath the surface. He reminded me of a volcano after years of eruptions of lava that heated and cooled. He stopped a short distance away, and I felt the heat billowing off of his body; straight from the Underworld.

"Declan."

"Balthazar."

Balthazar exhaled and plumes of smoke emitted from his mouth, and he rolled his shoulders. A faint crackling sounded, coming from his joints as he relaxed.

"I don't want to fight. I mean, it's unfair. There's so many of us," — he raised his arms, pointing at the row of glowing red eyes—his army, — "and only two of you." He pouted.

"True, but we have what you want."

"Yes, and because of that we won't kill you, even though Oleg already paid us handsomely."

I sighed. "Do you know where the sniveling bastard is?"

"I think he's rearranging your furniture and dusting your throne back home."

I snorted. "Of course." I sighed as we stared at each other. This wasn't going to end well. "I've already turned the wench; she has joined my kiss. I'd advise you and your mutts leave before I turn you all to dust. Oh, with the help of my trusty wolf." I thumbed at Winston behind me.

To say Balthazar was angry was an understatement. His skin erupted in lines of heated anger as the lava seeped out of his pores. I tasted the heat from where I stood and shuddered, hoping my skin wouldn't melt off my dead body.

"That's not what we agreed to. She is worth nothing if she's vampire."

"Precisely. I don't like it when others try to take what's rightfully mine. I found her first and needed everyone to know this. She. Is. Mine." I growled.

The row of glowing red eyes materialized as Balthazar's

army approached; each demon angrier than the one beside it.

I was looking forward to this. I moved my head from one side to the other, the distinct sound of clicking echoing in the chilled night.

"Now, Wolfie, show these dusty demons who's boss and send them back to their real master." I roared and dissolved into smoke.

Other vampires were afraid of my talents. Thank goodness I wasn't as crazy as the blood mist vampire I'd heard about ages ago. The vampire gods had blessed me with a few strengths; numb my victims with my bite, the usual strength that came with being a night hunter, and then where others only levitated, I dissolved into smoke. Which was what I did the moment Winston burst into his larger and scarier wolf form. He ripped into the demon who attacked him, a bite through his chest, and the demon exploded into a cloud of ash.

I darted for the next demon, raised my sharp talon through my smokey facade, and stabbed his chest. He exploded into ash before I changed my hand back into smoke.

Winston went for the next demon, who charged him like a crazed hellhound.

While we attacked and choked on ash powder, Balthazar roared in anger and started running away with his proverbial tail between his legs. I floated in his direction and materialized, landing on his back. He hit the ground with a solid *oof* escaping his lips. His scorching body burned my hands when I tried to stab him with my sharp claw. Then he'd heal quickly after each slash. And the bastard wiggled around like a worm.

"Lie still would you. I'm trying to kill you," I grunted as the demon continued to move out of my grasp.

"You won't get away with this, Declan. I've notified the others. We will find her and when we do, we're going to drain her of all her blood before eating her," he licked his lips, making a show of how much he'd enjoy doing that.

The threat he'd described filled me with a blinding rage. I anticipated his next move and swiped at his face; lava blood seeped out of his skin, and he pushed me off his body. He slammed his fist into me, and I flew a few paces backward.

Once on my feet, I charged at him again and we hit a sharp rock, then off the cliff. He landed in the sea first and started sinking. I kicked at him, hitting his head with my steel tip toe. The cut from his face leaked more lava, it cooled and hardened, causing him to sink faster. I'd never known demons could do that, but there were so many different types of demons I couldn't keep count. Each had their own specific set of skills and way of dying. This one seemed to hate water as lava continued oozing out of his wounds, cool, harden and weigh him down.

Balthazar fisted his frustration at me in so many foul signs. I'd had enough playing his stupid game and darted after him one last time. I struck him in his eye with my dark talon and ripped it out. I squished the pus-filled globe between my fingers while he screamed but all I heard was bubbles and the high-pitched sound of his blood hitting the water reminding me of a jet engine.

I watched him sink to the bottom of the ocean and smiled sinisterly. *Asshole!*

Once my head broke through the surface, I heard wolf-boy howl.

"There are more of them, Declan." Winston had part-changed into his human head to speak, otherwise all I'd hear were his barks. "They'll send more demons when they hear we've destroyed the others. We need help or they're going to destroy this city."

I darted out of the water and floated above Winston's head, then settled beside him. "Send Keith a message, tell him to get the girls out of there and to a hotel."

Chapter Twenty

DECLAN

My troubles seemed to mount with no idea how to solve them. I pissed the demons off, and if my sources were correct, more had escaped the Underworld. The Vampire Council would get angry because I wasn't handing Ursula over to them either, and Oleg would want my head shortly. Even with Winston by my side, dealing with them would end in disaster.

And then there was Lana. I wasn't ready to let go of her just yet. Unfortunately, I needed to tell her the truth. She could decide once she knew. I'd never used my vampiric wiles on a woman to like me. Either they did or they didn't. In all my relationships, I told them what I was and how things would be; and it was never exclusive. But this minx had somehow grabbed hold of my black heart and had wormed her way inside—jumpstarting it. My heart first started again with Ursula's kiss of life, but it was Lana who kept it going.

I groaned as I materialized and walked on the road, almost tripping myself. Beside me trotted my trusty steed

—Wolfie. I snickered at the thought, he'd kill me if I said that out loud. Winston needed to stay in his beast form or risk being locked away for public indecency. I would offer him my coat, but then he'd be a perverted exhibitionist flashing his manhood at unsuspecting passersby. I'd glimpsed at him before and happy to report he's well-endowed and would make any man or woman blush. But he was a private person, and although nudity was common among werewolves, he didn't enjoy strutting his stuff.

I rubbed behind his ear as we neared the hotel Keith had taken the ladies. Of all my troubles confronting Lana was the hardest.

My chest ached as I entered the lobby.

When the hotel manager approached, I stared him down. "There's nothing to see here," I said in my velvety smooth voice. "Go back to the front desk and wait for the next guest to arrive."

The manager's eyes glazed over, he bowed low and scurried away.

Anyone who approached us I glamoured. That included guests and other staff. They didn't need to see the big-ass wolf tailing me.

We rode the elevator to the penthouse suite and opened the door without knocking. Keith approached first, and I slammed my fist into his jaw. He crashed to the ground with a groan and nursed his jaw.

"Why isn't the door locked, Keith? I recall giving you specific instructions to keep the ladies safe. Yet I entered with no problems." I yelled at the driver squirming on the ground.

"What are you doing, Declan? Housekeeping was turning down the beds."

"I don't care, Ursula. The door needed to be locked." I closed the door behind Winston, who snarled at Keith.

"Sorry, I f-f-forgot," Keith stuttered.

Ursula and Lana ran to Keith and helped him to his feet.

The maid stared wide eyed at what had happened.

"Get out!" I yelled at her, watching her dash past me and left, closing the door gently behind her.

"What's up your butt?" Ursula said, folding her arms.

I pinched the bridge of my nose, counting to ten in Latin.

Winston aroooed beside me, egging me on.

"Fine," I grumbled. I had to just rip off the band-aid. "Lana," I started to say but stopped to swallow. She stared at me with longing, and I smelled her fear, along with my own. I was about to scare her again, but if she rejected me, then I'd know and I'd glamour the memory away. And Keith's. "Come sit with me," I said, my tone gentle as I calmed down. I approached the couch and sat.

Lana sat nervously beside me, turning her body slightly to face me.

Ursula sat on the coffee table once she found out Keith would live and no longer needed her nursing skills. Although I pictured her in a naughty nurse's outfit, her red hair wild against her shoulders, her breasts forced into a much smaller bra, making them voluptuous... hmmm. *Stop it!* I needed to focus.

I reigned in my fantasy and focused on Lana; sweet Lana, my little angel. *Crap.*

"Uhm—"

"Oh, enough already. Just tell her or I will."

"You know?" Lana pointed at Ursula.

"Yeah, and it's really not that bad," she grinned.

I ignored the naughty nurse. "Have you heard of vampires and werewolves—"

"Oh, is this what it's about. Oh, thank god," — she fell against the couch and giggled, — "I thought you were going to say something else."

I frowned at her. "Do you know I'm a vampire?"

"Yes," she giggled again, covering her mouth. The sound reverberated down my spine, making my cock stiffen.

"You're not afraid?" I asked carefully and moved my clothing so it didn't sit too tightly against my front.

She smiled sweetly and patted my hand that was now on her thigh. "I already knew what you were, silly. I mean, helloooo... there are supernatural monsters everywhere. How could I not know? Beautiful face, glowing blue or red eyes depending on your mood, not forgetting that marble body." She made a sound that mimicked a purr. "I might be inexperienced, but I'm not naïve."

The tension between my shoulders eased, and I sagged against the couch. "Good, at least that's settled then. What about you, Keith, knowing everything all right with you?"

Keith mumbled something unintelligible and gave us a thumbs up.

Bones broke, tendons snapped, and Winston exploded into his human form, blissfully uncaring about his nudity. I suspected he wanted to impress a certain naughty nurse.

"My god!" Ursula gawked; her hand covered her wide mouth.

Lana didn't blink.

"Thanks Watson, please cover your anaconda. You're embarrassing the tough vampire here."

"I'm going for a shower," he said as he wiped blood off his peck muscle and stared at Ursula.

"Do you need help with..." Ursula pointed at his midsection. "… with whatever you need cleaned?" she asked, feigning innocence.

"Actually, I'd love some. I'll ask the concierge to bring me some clothes."

"Yes, please do before the ladies drool everywhere." I cast a side-glance at Lana. "Close your mouth, dear." She chuckled and snuggled under my arm.

Ursula jumped up enthusiastically and followed Winston. But there was something I had to ask her.

"Oh, Ursula, wait before you enter Wolfie's lair. You have a choice to make, my sun goddess. What do you want to be when you grow up?"

"You going to change me?" she asked, her eyes flitting from me then to Winston. "Do you mean wolf or vampire?"

I nodded.

She grinned, and her cheeks reddened. "I love wolves, I really do, but I love vampires more. But… I don't know now. Can I think about it?"

"Sure, but not too long. There are more crazies after you and we need to sort you out before they know you're still human."

She squealed, clapped hands and jumped onto Winston's back. God, that girl was something else. First she kissed me and now Winston. Although I couldn't blame her, he was dashing under all that macho fur.

I squeezed Lana's thigh, and she shrieked. I pushed my hand under her skirt and higher up her thigh, revealing more tender skin.

"So…" I started, needed her to know my intensions. I didn't know if she wanted to stay with me. And the possibility of her coming back with me to America was real, I wanted her to join me. But the threat of her getting bored with me was a reality, or I might tire. Although things might be different. She was the first woman I'd wanted to be faithful to. She filled my mind all the time, and I wanted to do a lot of dirty things to her. I licked my lips.

My hand moved farther up her leg until I reached that sweet core and pushed my fingers under her panties. She sucked in a deep breath and slouched lower on the couch, opening her legs for me.

Moaning to my left made me hiss, Keith was watching, and he had his hand over the front of him. As much as I loved flaunting my body, I didn't want anyone seeing Lana.

I picked her up and carried her to the second bedroom and kicked the door closed with my foot. She held onto my shoulders and nuzzled into my neck. Her warmth made me shudder in anticipation.

"Are you ready for me, Lana?" I breathed as I gently lay her on the bed.

She nodded, her big green eyes staring into mine. I removed my coat, but she stopped me by climbing onto her knees and pulled me closer. She removed my coat and threw it on the floor, then slowly unbuttoned my shirt. She pulled it out of my pants and pushed it off my shoulders. Then she ran her fingers up the ridges of my muscles and flicked my nipple.

"Ow," I said as I feigned injury.

"Oh, rubbish. Don't be such a baby." Lana snaked her arms around my neck and pulled me closer, our lips touching, her tongue needing mine. She kissed me hungrily while my hands started undressing her. I hissed when she pulled away. She shimmied out of her skirt and removed her top, standing on the bed wearing matching underwear.

I whistled.

She climbed off the bed, placed her hands on the edge and pushed her ass against the front of me. I slapped her ass cheeks; she yelped, and I yanked her underwear off. My pants came off too, and I held onto those hips. I was so quick she didn't have a chance to run away.

"What do you want, Lana?"

"You," she breathed seductively.

My cock twitched, I pushed up against her so she could feel how hard I was. She moaned as I rubbed her back, unclipping her bra, then lifting her hands to free herself of the device.

She stood bent over, practically begging for me to take her.

"I want to hear what you want." I covered her back with my front and cupped her breasts.

"I want to scream your name, Declan. Do naughty things to me. I want you." She turned around, forcing me to stand up. She rocked onto her toes and cupped my face. "I don't understand what this is, but I enjoy being near you. Maybe you've used your vampire powers on me, hypnotizing me into liking you. But all I know is I want to be with you."

"Even though I'm a vampire."

She nodded. "Even though you are one."

"And I'm not tricking you, angel, this," — I motioned between her and me, — "is all real."

Her smile lit up her face upon hearing I had used none of my machinations on her.

Now that the hard part was over. I could ask the other thing burning in my mind. Most of the human girls I'd messed around with yearned for my love bite, the one that made them my fledgling forever. But I never did. Did this sweet, yet not so innocent, woman want that, too? She already knew what I was, was it something she wanted?

"Do you want my forever bite?"

"Honestly, I don't know." She chewed on her bottom lip as she mulled it over. "But you're leaving soon, and I didn't want to just invite myself into your life, but—"

"Do you want to come home with me, to America?"

She nodded. "I'm alone here. I hardly see my dad—"

"It's settled then. When this crap is over, you pack whatever you need and let your dad know you're leaving town." My chest filled with hope and desire. I leaned into her and kissed delicately, not wanting the evening to end.

Chapter Twenty-One

LANA

My body thrummed at his touch, and I couldn't wait for him to sink deep inside. He pushed me up the bed while we kissed; as if he were too afraid of letting go. I laid down with him on top and between my legs; I felt my arousal drip between my legs and my cheeks heated. I was sure he felt the wetness on his knee.

Declan moved a hand between us and reached for my slick slit and moaned as he broke the kiss. "So needy." He nipped my lower lip and smiled seductively. "I have a remedy for that." He kissed the column of my neck and I felt him freeze near my pulse.

I swallowed hard. The thought of his bite sent a sensual thrill down my spine, but I wasn't sure. I wanted him to bite me; it was exciting, but it scared me. Maybe he was pushing my boundaries to see if I trusted him—I did —turning my head, I allowed him access to what he wanted.

"No, my sweet girl, you haven't told me you wanted it. And if I bite you now, you wouldn't feel anything else."

I faced him, my heart racing, not quite understanding what he meant. "How come?"

"My bite is potent; it will numb your body for at least an hour. And what I'm about to do to you, it's best if you feel everything," he smirked.

I smiled as a shiver ran through me; I ached to feel every inch of him.

"One day," I said cautiously.

"One day," he repeated with mischievous eyes. "But now," he kissed down my body, sucking in a nipple. "Let's enjoy each other's bodies," he said, grazing the other bud with sharp teeth. Arching my back, giving him more of myself, then he continued lower.

Declan kissed down my stomach until he reached my mound. Sliding his hands underneath my ass, he raised me off the bed and kissed those lips like he just kissed me, carefully, lovingly but forcefully. He teased, licked, and sucked. He continued his punishing pattern with his tongue, piercing my slick folds and driving me mad. An aching need burst through me like lightening as he brought me over. The moment he entered a finger I flew over the edge; my fingers digging holes into the mattress, and I screamed his name.

He slowed his rhythm but continued that teasing, kissing, sucking and hummed, which sent another shocking thrill through my body making my stomach muscles tighten as another orgasm struck me. I grabbed his head to keep him where he was until my arms fell away and my legs shook.

"Gods, your body is so…" He shook his head. "I'm at a loss for words. Imagine that?" he grinned. "This was what your first time was meant to be like."

I smacked dry lips together and tried to swallow. Finally, I found my voice. "It was,"—I licked my lips again, —

"amazing. Wow!" I felt my cheeks flush and when the bed moved, my eyes shot open.

Declan hovered above me, his piercing gaze boring into my soul. "You ready for me, darling?"

"Uh-huh," I smiled and clung to his shoulders.

He slowly eased inside, allowing me to get used to his girth. The rhythm of him sliding into me relaxed my body as I savored each stroke, each touch as I offered myself to him. I wanted him to feel that I wanted this, that I wanted him.

Yes, I'd known he was a vampire all along and hoped he wouldn't hurt me. Vampires rarely killed their victims these days, although there was a murder the other day. But Declan didn't hurt me. He had a temper. But they all did.

My stomach tightened at the sensation of his continuous rhythm, burning a need within. My desire flared through me, heating my veins, and felt as though I would combust.

Soft whimpers escaped my mouth as I savored his delicious touch.

Declan grunted above me. I opened my eyes and he smiled, his eyes glowing red. He lowered his head and kissed my neck, licked my ear lobe then his lips found mine.

He thrusted harder, my mouth opened, and he darted his tongue inside. With each thrust, his tongue ravaged mine. The feeling below and the feeling in my mouth felt strange and contradictory, but the combination was a burst of sensual explosions shooting through me.

I grabbed his ass and met his thrust with my own. He groaned in the kiss as his movements became uncoordinated. His kissing became tender, but his powerful thrusts harder and it pushed us over the edge together—our orgasms exploding at the same time. He pumped his seed into me, the heat of it sent another burst of sensations through me, and I squeezed around him.

He slowed his thrusts to short bursts until he stopped and collapsed on top of me. I wrapped my legs around his waist and my arms around his shoulders and clung to him. It felt so strange, yet safe and comforting. I could stay like this forever.

Chapter Twenty-Two

URSULA

I stared at wolf-boy unsure whether this was the right thing to do but my body screamed hell yes! I gauged his reaction to me following him into the bathroom, and I felt like a deer caught in a hunter's trap. His predatory gaze sent a zing of sensations down my spine, which coiled in my core, setting my panties on fire. I was going to die loving his touch.

My attraction to Declan was an infatuation. I scratched that need by kissing him and realizing there wasn't anything there.

But Winston was... he was absolutely different, and my heart ached whenever he wasn't near. I was a crazy fool in my mid-thirties, who had a crush on a man I'd hoped would become more than just that.

Winston was my height, which was short for a man, but built strong and powerful. His naked chest heaved up and down as he stared at me, his green eyes piercing every inch of my body, mind, and soul.

Slowly, I removed my shirt, then my pants and stood in my underwear; at least the garments matched.

Winston approached, butterflies flew out of their cage in my womb, and I shivered in anticipation. He pressed his hands on either side of my hips and squeezed the curves. Closing his eyes, his nostrils flared—no doubt smelling me —then pressed his forehead against mine.

"It's been a while for me," he whispered so softly I barely heard him.

"We can go slowly." I reassured him and wrapped my arms around his shoulders and pressed my body against his.

He moved his head to my shoulder and kissed, sending pleasure through my core, my arousal making my panties moist.

"I don't know how or why, but shit... you do it for me." I confessed.

I felt him nod as his right hand moved down my body and laced his thumb in my panties, pulling them down. I stepped out of them and unclasped my bra. He sucked one nipple into his mouth and pulled, sending another sharp shooting pain to my core followed by another mini shock wave, tearing whimpers from me.

His hand moved lower and cupped my bare mound, and a deep growl reverberated from his chest. His fingers found my slick folds, and he hissed as he played with me. I spread my legs for him, leaning closer and cupped his face. I pressed my lips to his and tasted him. The moment his tongue found mine, he inserted two fingers, making me gasp. He pumped his fingers into me, tearing sounds of ecstasy from my mouth.

"I don't want to go slowly," he growled, removing his fingers. "I want to fuck you hard and fast, shower and wash your body, then do it all over again."

I nodded, struggling for words. That sounded perfect, but I couldn't speak—I could barely stand.

Winston picked me up and carried me to the bed, and as my butt touched the mattress, he hovered above me. He stroked his hardness, then pressed it against my folds, nudging inside.

"Are you ready for me?"

"Yes," I whimpered.

He rammed into my heated core over and over, grunting and growling. The movements were so savage and brutal, yet pleasurable. I came within the first few seconds, sending my heart racing, my core tightening and foul words flying out of my mouth.

Winston didn't stop. He was an animal. He pumped into me so hard and fast, hitting right to the end; I felt every stroke as if he were going slowly. I didn't understand it myself, but it felt heavenly. Sometimes one just needed that animal-like movement to get it out of your system, then go slower the next round. And if Winston hadn't done it for a while, I doubted he'd last long.

The man continued his controlled thrusts, grunting into the nape of my neck while I clung to his body. When I met his movement with my own, he pummeled into me. After my third orgasm, he found his release. I squeezed, milking him.

I felt used and slightly sore down there, but it was amazing.

Slowly, he slipped out and fell on the bed beside me. Sweat dripped down the sides of his face and the corners of his mouth curved into a smile that made me smile.

"That was fucking amazing," I hummed as I moved onto my side and caressed his chest; he had fine hairs you could only see up close. His muscles twitched where I touched, and his cock stirred again. "Again?" I stared at his anaconda as Declan had so delicately put. I suspected

Declan might be large if the bulge in his pants was anything to go by, Winston was holy-crap-where-is-it-going-to-go big. No wonder I ached deliciously.

"Honey, you have no idea. But I need a shower and I'd love to wash that body of yours."

I grinned and sat up. "Lead the way, wolf-man."

Chapter Twenty-Three

DECLAN

I gave Winston a side glance and arched an eyebrow. "What did you do to her?" I watched Ursula cringe with each step.

He shrugged. "Nothing you wouldn't do."

"True, but she can barely walk." I stifled a laugh. "How many times did you go at it?"

"I lost count, but I'd do it again," Ursula said, carefully sitting on a pillow.

I laughed as Lana hugged me from behind. I pulled her to my side and kissed the top of her head.

"Okay, I have a plan." Winston raised a bushy eyebrow. "Don't give me that look, you know what the plan is." I gave a wolfish grin.

I explained what I wanted to do, and Ursula paled.

"At the same time? What will happen to me?"

"My dear, it's exactly what you want, and need. I've spoken with the Oracle from Chicago, and she's the one who suggested the idea. It's the only way to keep the demons and the Vampire Council at bay. And we're running out of time. Both will arrive shortly." I'd spoken with Alex who sat on the Vampire Council. He agreed he'd meet with me, and that Ursula was priceless, and nobody should take possession of her. She was not a commodity one traded or used. She was a Child of the Sun and should be treated like royalty.

I watched her swallow as she composed herself. Finally, she nodded and stood. "Okay, let's do this."

I'd spoken with Winston while the girls slept and asked whether he wanted to turn Ursula into one of his kind or did he want her as his mate. There was a difference and depending on what we did could change her.

My conversation with the Oracle had fueled ideas, and she had narrowed down two possibilities with similar steps but different outcomes.

We would bond Ursula to each of us, which would preserve her precious blood. She'd live longer and make her physically more powerful. We would only need a few drops of her blood and perform our various rituals binding her to us in the metaphysical realm. We only needed her blood, but she wouldn't need ours.

Or, we'd both drink from her, then give her our blood to consume in order to turn her into a wolf and/or vampire at the same time. We'd have to wait and see which virus destroyed her blood first or if she'd accept both.

In either case, she would have the werewolves and vampires on her side, and we'd destroy the demons together. The Lord of the Underworld would have to fight with his fledglings if he craved Ursula for himself. But since I hadn't heard from Victor, I surmised he had little or no interest in our redhead, and his demons were acting on their own accord. Or worse, it was Victor's brother, Seth, who had sent the demons after her.

I'd also spoken with Salvador, who had a demon as a

pet, and they had called him to war. Salvador, being a powerful vampire and had fathered two vampire sons after he'd turned, had ordered his demon to remain and if the leader of the demons wanted him, he had to fight Salvador first. The leader had left Salvador's demon alone, which made me chuckle. But Salvador warned me the masses were coming and we should brace ourselves.

In the meantime, Salvador had informed his son, Léon who was Master Vampire of Sterling Meadow, of what was happening.

I breathed a sigh of relief as my problems were slowly diminishing. I didn't need to breathe; the motion of my chest rising and falling felt good as the tension floated away.

With Lana on one side, a powerful redhead on the other, hopefully the demons would go away spilling no blood.

My final problem was Oleg—he was mine alone and I couldn't wait to rip into that conniving miscreant.

Chapter Twenty-Four

URSULA

My nerves were about to bubble out my chest. I had Winston on my left and Declan on my right. Both sets of eyes glowed, and I almost peed in my pants. I didn't know what to expect. It was exciting but scary.

Declan had explained that they would rather bond me to each of them. I reluctantly agreed.

When I'd first asked Declan to turn me into one of his darling night hunters, it was something I dreamed of and excited about. The more I thought about it, I realized I didn't want to stop eating food and start drinking blood. I shuddered at the thought. And I'd miss the sun too much.

Instead, through their bonding, I'd have both the wolves and vampires on my side but without changing into either creature. I felt relieved. I'd still be living to a godawful age, and would die if either got hurt.

Yeah, I was fooling myself. It petrified me.

"Relax," Declan purred beside me. My hand was in both of his and he kissed the top. "In my bonding, I must feed from you, then say the words to complete the ritual. It's when our souls join in the metaphysical realm, tying you to me. It's not like creating baby vampires I become their master, this will be a partnership."

The wrinkles between my eyes deepened as I recalled what I'd read. "But," I stuttered and my eyes landed on Lana.

Declan shook his head in warning. "It's all right, pumpkin. I can bind many to me," he said with a wicked grin.

"Okay." I tried to smile reassuringly but my cheeks quivered.

"I know we've just met, but mine isn't like Declan's." Winston started to say then stepped closer to me. He picked up my other hand and kissed the top. When his eyes found mine, they glowed a green/yellow color and his fangs elongated. "I only mate once in my life—"

"But—"

"There will be no but's," — he pressed his sharp claw to my lips, — "and it would honor me to have you as mine. And even though you'll be bound to Declan, your body and heart are mine." He growled the last part as his eyes flitted to Declan, who bowed in agreement.

"So you've never found your true mate?"

He shook his head and sighed sadly. "I'd been this fool's errand boy for ages and well," he shrugged, "I was never looking. But you, sweet girl, you are the piece I'd always been missing." He caressed my cheek carefully. "Usually when a human survived a vicious bite from a were-animal they'd turn into that animal. But in my bonding, I only need a sip of your blood and I'll ensure my potent saliva won't mix with your blood. You will remain human while your soul will be that of a wolf. You will smell like a wolf to others, and your senses may even enhance, but you will remain a human."

I nodded numbly, feeling only slightly better. I exhaled sharply and nodded.

"Winston will do his thing first before I bite you and say the words. Thereafter you will become numb. My bite," — he cast a quick glance in Lana's direction, but she didn't flinch. Either she was braver than me, or she wasn't completely aware of what was happening. — "My bite will numb your body for a short while. Hopefully, during that time, both bonds will be in effect."

He didn't mention he'd already bitten me, and I was only numb for a few short minutes, and I wondered if it was for Lana's benefit. He cupped my cheeks and kissed me delicately.

"And Watson is right, you are his, but you and I can communicate secretly," Declan whispered and winked before stepping aside to give Winston space.

Winston growled because he had heard and enveloped me in his arms. I melted against his body, felt his heat, while his heartbeat against my chest. He was just as nervous as I was, which relieved me. He kissed me with a fiery passion that burned from within. I hadn't noticed it before because so much was happening, but this felt right. Being with Winston and having him hold me like he did felt like home. I felt like I finally belonged.

My eyes closed as his fur spread over his naked body and my fingers combed his hair. The next moment my fingers caressed his skin as he shifted back, and his fiery breath hit my neck. A sharp pain struck me, then his heat poured through me. He picked me up and carried me to the bed where he made sweet love to me as delicately as possible.

He filled his strokes with tender love while he continued to sip my blood. I felt his hands on my body, him inside my body, but I also felt swirls of something surrounding us. I heard his wolf's growl in my ears, and I saw his large animal body rubbing up against mine. It was a surreal out-of-body experience, but it didn't scare me.

My heart rate settled into a comfortable rhythm that didn't leave me hyperventilating, and it was in time with Winston's. When he pushed us delicately over the edge, our orgasms felt like the sun had burst through the dark cloudy skies and reached for our naked bodies with its heat, surrounding us with its comforting golden light.

My heart burst with love, and I felt how happy Winston was, too. He'd lived for years alone. He hadn't found the one he wanted to bond with, yet he'd only known me a few days. But, as short as our courtship was, it felt right. My heart was happy, my body ecstatic, while my mind and soul were content.

As we came down from our lovemaking high, an icy hand reached for mine, pulling me out from under Winston.

Declan lay on my other side, fully clothed, and kissed the my neck.

Winston kept me warm on the other side while the vampire neared, sinking his venomous fangs into my neck.

I felt the instant pull of the vampire's powers and I grabbed Winston for dear life. It was the complete opposite of what I'd just experienced; Winston was gentle and relaxed, Declan was forceful and immediate.

Declan's power swirled around me like I'd just opened pandora's box; a combination of different things hitting me at once. A cool power wrapped itself around my head, warm thrumming power hooked into my heart, while another delicate, not quite there, fangs sinking into my flesh.

Declan drank from me, his vampire power swirled around me, then when he released me, he whispered foreign words I would never remember. It felt like a bubble popped in my face, my body pulled in his direction as my soul bound by chains latched onto him. Well, that's what it felt like. Whether that really happened in the metaphysical world, I'd never know.

Winston whined beside me, licking my face as he had partially shifted; his larger wolf's head rubbing against my cheek as the vampire venom set its hooks within me, leaving me numb and senseless.

Declan kissed the wound to seal the bond and said something else. By then my eyes rolled into the back of my head, my body stilled, and I think I died just a little.

On one side I felt warm and cozy, while the other side I felt frozen.

Then I embraced the darkness.

Chapter Twenty-Five

DECLAN

"She looks dead," Lana shrieked beside me.

"At least she's quiet."

Lana slapped my chest.

"I'm joking," I chuckled. "It will be okay, she will look like that for a few more minutes, then she'll be her usual chirpier self."

"Promise?" Lana asked carefully, her green eyes misty.

"I promise." I squeezed my minx against my body and kissed the top of her head. "That blood of hers is quite delicious. I'd love to taste her again—"

Winston snarled.

"With your permission, of course. I would never dare otherwise. We must get ready. I feel Alex's approach. He'd be arriving alone, but you never know with those devils and their machinations."

Lana giggled. "Aren't you like that?"

"Sometimes, maybe." I shrugged nonchalantly.

Winston grunted.

"Enough, Watson. Now shower and get ready, you smell

like a wet dog. We need to save one of our own and go home."

"Declan?"

"Yes, honey. What can I do for you?"

Lana stared longingly at Ursula and bit her bottom lip, then turned to gaze at me once more. "Will I be your only... Uh... The only woman in your life? I know you bound her to you to keep her safe but—"

"Do I want to bind you to me, too?"

She nodded slowly. "I don't want to drink blood and any of that yucky stuff, and I don't want to turn into a bat. But," she glanced down at Ursula again. "Maybe when we get to your home, I could make my decision."

I chuckled at the bat comment. "Whatever you want, my dear." I squeezed her waist. Sometime during the last few days I'd fallen for this angel at my side, and I'd do anything to keep her with me. I would suffer if she aged and died, but I'd be the luckiest vampire alive if I bound her to me. "I'm in no hurry, sweet angel. Let me know when the time is right."

"Okay." She bit her lip again, mulling it over. "But let's first get out alive."

"Oh Declan, what have you done?" Alex said through a sigh, casting a glare my way that would set a human on fire. "The Vampire Council will not be pleased about this." He held Ursula by her shoulders, no doubt testing if she was a human. "Her blood remains pure?"

"Yes," I licked blood from my thumb for effect. "I had another snack on the way here to test."

Ursula sat in a chair, staring wide eyed at the handsome

bloke. For as long as I'd known Alex, he'd always been single. But that didn't mean he never had someone in his bed. His unbrushed blond hair still looked as if he did it on purpose, while his green eyes sparkled with power. If I was afraid of him, just imagine how scary he was to others.

"Do you mind if I taste you, dear?" Alex purred and Ursula blushed, nodding now that she could move some of her body parts. No doubt his beauty had left her dumbstruck.

I chuckled while Winston stifled a growl. He was not pleased, understandably.

Surrounding our little group was an infestation of demons. A thick dark wall of smoking bodies slamming their heat into us. I wished I could manipulate water and spray them to watch them sizzle.

Alex straddled our woman, which offered her the chance to grab hold of his waist. Winston's lips curled over his sharp human teeth—he was already so protective of her. As fated mates, perhaps now Winston would take that stick out of his ass and relax. But the way he stared possessively at Ursula, I doubted it.

Alex held her head to one side and sank his fangs into her delicious skin. My cock twitched, and I dared not tear my eyes away. I squeezed Lana's side, bringing her closer to me.

Alex hummed his satisfaction and cleaned the wound. He sat up, smacking his lips together, and faced us. His eyes glowed yellow. I almost stepped backward. If you knew what was good for you, you never stepped back from a Master Vampire on the Council. My jaw dropped, Lana gasped beside me, while Winston grabbed Ursula to cradle her in his arms.

"Okay." Alex raised his hands and yelled louder for the

demons to hear. "She's bound to Declan and is part of his kiss, and she is part-wolf. No supernatural being, and no demon, may lay a hand on her. If you wish to fight, I'll call Victor who I'm sure didn't allow this."

Balthazar's second in command approached, snapped his fingers, and the dark wall disappeared in a cloudy dust of smoke.

Lana waved her hand in front of her face and coughed. Then when that didn't work, she buried her face in my jacket.

The wind from the southwest blew the cloud away, and I sucked in the sea breeze between my teeth. I would miss this beautiful city when we headed back inland to Krystal Creek.

Although our time was short, so much had happened that it felt like we were here the full month. I'd tasted the various flavors Cape Town offered; Ursula found out what she truly was, I gained an angel at my side, while Winston found his true mate. Everybody had their happily ever after.

We had converged on top of Table Mountain as it was safer for the humans if we isolated ourselves. And the space was enormous enough to accommodate the demons.

"My name is Osmodeus and I need to taste for myself. I promise not to hurt her, but I must know for certain. And just so you know, Seth sent us—Victor's brother."

When I nodded, Osmodeus approached Ursula with care.

I had to admit it, Osmodeus restrained the urge to use his power on her and wondered what his gift was. His skin was dark and unblemished. He had no hard cracks as Balthazar had, yet the air crackled with electricity that made my arms pebble.

Osmodeus caressed Ursula's skin and pushed his face

into her neck. He smelled her skin and glanced at Winston. "I smell your wolf on her." He sniffed on her other side and glanced at me. "And I smell you vampire."

What shocked me, instead of finding himself a sweet spot at that pale column. He gently took her arm in his hands, and she relaxed into Winston, who sat on the chair with her on his lap.

Osmodeus brought her wrist to his mouth, to his sharp teeth, and bit into her.

Ursula moaned, and I smelled her arousal—which affected me. My pants shrunk near my front once more and although I appreciated watching, it would seem I had a direct line to her pleasure points.

I stared at Winston who nodded, understanding what was happening and fought his instincts to kill the demon for touching her or if he should pleasure himself instead.

"Christ, you're an incubus." I rubbed the front as my hardened erection strained against my tight jeans.

It left Alex aroused, and he turned around, no longer able to watch.

Osmodeus slurped as he drank from her wrist. A faint golden glow surrounded his body, and he finally unclenched his teeth from her slender wrist. He licked her wound, and it healed instantly. He gently placed her hand in her lap and shuddered, causing the glow to brighten more yellow, then it faded. Once he'd licked his lips for the tenth time, he finally spoke.

"Okay, you're right. If we fought over her, nobody would win. We would tear her apart. It will piss off Seth, but I'd like to offer him the chance to taste her for himself, but only once she's home with you. I'm sure he would come to the same conclusion I did. And I agree to the treaty.

Crushing her would be the last thing anybody wants," Osmodeus said with sadness laced in his words.

I did a double take to ensure it was the same demon who had wanted to slaughter us earlier. I watched him stare at Ursula like his life depended on it, then jerking awake he bowed down low and disappeared in a cloud of ash.

"Well, that was strange." I turned to Alex, who seemed as conflicted as I. "I think we've overstayed our welcome. Perhaps we need to head back home and finalize everything with my new position."

Alex nodded and started walking towards the edge of the mountain.

Once we reached the vehicle at the bottom, Keith had paled and gripped the steering wheel for dear life.

Winston carried Ursula, who was dreaming something erotic because her arousal still filled the air.

I pulled Lana closer to me. The silly girl didn't want to remain in the car and was stunned into silence about what she'd just witnessed.

"Are you okay?" I whispered near the shell of her ear. "You're awfully quiet."

"I'm just processing everything. The most excitement I've ever had was when I passed a car accident." She shuddered and cuddled closer under my arm.

"Fascinating," I said dryly. "But this is the life I lead. You need to speak now before we leave. Are you sure you want to join me?" The question was serious, and she needed to answer after thoughtful consideration.

"I am. You need to understand I may not be fragile, but I need time to get used to things."

"Understood." I kissed her temple. "Pack a bag, grab your identification so we can leave before the night is through. The smells here are getting to me." I chuckled, casting an eye at Winston who snarled at me. I hissed back.

Chapter Twenty-Six

URSULA

Lana and I packed our bags and boarded Declan's private airplane. I'd arranged with a lawyer friend to ensure the furniture in my house moved to a storage facility and she would help sell the property. There were too many painful memories, and I hated staying there anyway.

It felt like we flew for thousands of hours to the US, but thank heavens we were on a private plane and there were beds. Well, Declan and Lana had the bed. Winston and I snuggled on the couch. It was heaven in the sky.

Filled with panic and dread about what I'd done, but if I really thought about it, I didn't feel any different from what I did before Winston and Declan bound me to them. I would however catch stray thoughts or words from Winston and finish his sentence. The only thing I got from Declan was a powerful zap when he reached his climax.

If anyone asked if I regretted my decisions? No, absolutely not. This was what I wanted. My life needed more, and if I hadn't met Declan, I'd never have known about my heritage. And, if any supernatural had found out about it,

I'd be dead, anyhow. So no, I had a permanent boyfriend and a funny employer who still suffered from teenager mood swings, but I'd learn his ways soon enough. And I had a best friend for some girl talk.

We were heading to Declan's new hometown with our futures brighter than what they were before, and I couldn't wait to start the rest of my life with the hunky wolf-man by my side.

Chapter Twenty-Seven

LANA

Declan snuggled into my neck, and my pulse thundered. The naughty vampire still made me nervous, even though I lay spent and unable to move my body. It would seem he never got enough of me. But then again, neither did I.

He moaned as he slung his arm over my stomach, pulling me closer to him.

"There's no way I can get any closer to you, Declan." I stifled a giggle. "And besides, I need a shower. All I smell is my sweat and our lovemaking."

He growled low and dirty. "I like that word, lovemaking. My dear, you are the only woman to say that to me. For that alone, I will love you forever."

To say my heart stopped was an understatement. But it did. I felt like a mouse caught in the bear's trap. He'd caught me off guard, and even though I was too afraid to say it, I might have felt it, too.

I kissed his nose to make up for the long stretch of silence.

"Give me time. I'm thinking about everything and although I can't say it yet, I love being around you."

"That's all a man can ask." His lips found mine once more, and I melted against him.

I loved him, strangely, but this was for the rest of my life...

Chapter Twenty-Eight

DECLAN

I watched Lana sashay towards the bathroom, I'd never tire of her sweet ass swaying in front of me. She was a ripe, juicy plum for my taking.

I joined Lana in the shower; I washed her soft, warm skin and ensured she was squeaky clean. She washed my body, and all I did was kiss her. She had complained she was a little sensitive and sore and didn't want to push her luck. Once home I'd make sure she couldn't walk for a week, but for now, I'd leave her be.

Once dressed, we joined the lovebirds in front and ate; Winston enjoyed his medium rare steak while I had a glass of warm blood. My hostess was a regular donor of mine, and I rewarded her handsomely with money and my award-winning smile.

By the time the captain said we were about to descend, I'd already made the necessary arrangements to meet Léon, Master Vampire of Sterling Meadow. It was a formal greeting where we introduced ourselves. Since we were going to be neighbors and our towns were relatively close enough to warrant such festivities, the Vampire Council had agreed, and Alex would join us to ensure a smooth process.

I liked Léon; he was fair, smart, and kind. But I also knew others had confused his kindness for weakness and had never surfaced again. The ancient vampire might be generous, but still lethal.

The plane landed smoothly, and it was still dark outside. We climbed into our vehicle and drove to our residence. Winston had arranged for the removal company to pack our items from my old residence and moved us into the new mansion. The place was a monster.

Our previous house was a double story in Las Vegas, where I was the second-in-command to the Master Vampire there. My powers had grown, and I wasn't a tyrant, and he'd offered his referral to the Council, suggesting I'd make an excellent master.

Krystal Creek was a small town in the middle of the States. It had a master for a brief period then not again, and since the town had grown exponentially they wanted me to take residency tonight. There was much to be done.

And then there was Oleg. The blood thirsty barbarian who I regretted turning. Many years ago, he was my friend and had always known what I was. As vikings we plundered, killed and took what we wanted and on our last trip they attacked us, and Oleg needed me.

I'd bitten him and he'd turned into my fledgling, but his ravenous appetite for blood only increased and he wanted more. I'd tried to sate his hunger and tried to keep him under control, but he was a savage. There was nothing I could do to stop him.

When he saw how I'd moved into power within the vampire lines, he too wanted what I had and followed me. I tried to guide him, but he was ungovernable.

When he'd heard about my new status as master, he wanted that too. And somehow, he had requested the Vampire Council offer him the seat should anything happen to me—especially since I didn't have my kiss in place.

If Oleg was in town, I would rip his eyes out along with disemboweling him for the trouble he put me through.

Winston drove through the open wrought-iron gates and up the winding driveway.

The girls giggled in the backseat and gasped when they saw the large house.

"Holy cow," Lana said.

"What in the world? Declan, this place is beautiful," Ursula marveled.

"It is, isn't it?" I smirked and cast my eyes at the immense mansion before us.

Krystal Creek was an old mining town and as the world changed, so had the residents. More people moved here because of the outdoor living, employment increased, followed by more schools and another hospital. The shifters took to it because of the forests surrounding the town. And those wanting the nightlife escaped to Sterling Meadow for the evening.

The house we now called home was one of the oldest houses built by the man who had once owned the mines. At a quick glance you'd think of the Winchester house, but it didn't have as many rooms or staircases leading to locked doors. They'd painted the triple story home a pale yellow and refurbished it. The circle driveway held a fountain in the middle. The house was a classic, yet modern. It was perfect for us.

Winston slowed the car, and the girls jumped out before he even parked. I chuckled at their excitement, and it left my chest warm.

In the previous house I shared with Winston, it was only the two of us, but with the girls I knew they'd bring an extra flavor of excitement into our new lives.

Alex parked behind us and nodded curtly, followed by Léon and two of his men.

"Welcome," Léon said, and stopped as he waited for me to exit the vehicle. "This is Sawyer and Marc, my shifter protection."

"Thanks for coming over so soon. I thought it best to get the introductions out of the way and discuss Oleg."

Léon nodded, his deep blue eyes sparkling with humor. His eyes flitted to Alex, then back to me. "He tried to enter Sterling Meadow without announcing his arrival in my town, and I've banned him. We will kill him if he tries again. And all the shifters know what he tried to do to you with the demon's help." He shook his head. "None of it was necessary, yet," he shrugged nonchalantly, "here we are."

"Right," I said and headed towards the house. "And that's Watson." I thumbed behind me.

"It's actually Winston." I heard him say as I entered the house. The men joked about something. No doubt Winston had rolled his eyes or mouthed I was crazy.

The men entered the house and headed for the study, and their shocked expressions mirrored mine. In the living room were the carcasses of wild animals nailed to the walls with a message in blood; *'You're next.'*

"Right, thank heavens the girls darted upstairs, or we'd all be deaf from their screams. Winston, help take these down. We can continue our discussion in the library." I pointed the way while Winston, Sawyer, and Marc removed the dead animals.

"The Vampire Council have a kill order out on Oleg. If he comes here again, you have permission to kill him without our presence," Alex said as he glanced at the books on the shelves.

"That's good to know." The last thing I needed was the Council turning me to ash over Oleg's death.

The rest of the hour we discussed how Léon and I could work together. He even came prepared with a business proposal. Since I had mines on my side and he had shifters, more would move to my town to open the mines for precious gems or gold—whichever was found—and we'd share the profit.

Alex approved the proposal, I agreed, and Léon shook my hand. The two vampires left, leaving me alone with the girls and Winston.

I wanted to show Lana the grounds before the sun rose, but before I reached the stairs, a noise outside caught me off guard. It sounded like a mini explosion.

"Don't go outside," Winston yelled as he jumped four steps at a time, landing softly on padded feet beside me. "I can smell him," he snarled, his hackles rising.

"I know," I patted his head, "I smell him too." I exhaled. "He waited for the others to leave." It was now, or he'd just keep coming back like a nasty rash. "Let's get this over with."

Footsteps sounded down the stairs as the ladies asked what was happening.

"Stay upstairs, please. I don't want the bastard to see either of you." He no doubt already knew of their existence because of the alluring smell they gave off, which left me angered.

I grabbed the dagger I kept near the entrance and saw my glowing eyes in the mirror. When I opened the door, I found Oleg standing near the fountain with a few demons scattered around him.

The tall blond man with glowing blue eyes had the audacity to smirk. "I like your new place, Declan. But it suits me better." He stretched his broad shoulders, readying for a fight.

"How about this, send your puppies home and just you and I fight?" I descended the steps and stopped a short distance from him. "Nobody else has to get hurt. This is between you and me, anyway."

He shook his head. "Seth wants the girl."

"I've already spoken with Osmodeus and he agrees nobody should touch her."

"That's not what Seth wants."

"Fine, if you win, there's nobody here to stop you. But they need to stay back." I pointed at the demons, then turned to face Winston and whispered. "Get the girls out of here." I couldn't risk Oleg getting his grubby hands on either of them—and certainly not Seth. Victor was Lord of the Underworld. His brother was a vile creature and would torture them relentlessly. Even if Oleg wasn't here for Lana, one whiff of her and he'd take her any way he wanted.

Winston darted inside again like the smart wolf he was.

"Right," I cracked my knuckles, grateful that a cloud of dust didn't emit from my pores. I hadn't fought with another vampire in years and couldn't wait to teach this one a lesson. "Where were we?" I called him over with a claw. "It's just you and me, baby vampire. Send your pets home."

Oleg waved the demons away, and they went poof into clouds of smoke. He pushed off the fountain and stalked me. He neared as I stepped closer to him. I didn't wait for him to reach me; I lunged at him swiping my sharp claws down the front of his chest slicing through his clothing and drawing first blood.

He hissed; I hissed back, and my fangs elongated.

We circled each other. His hands morphed into claws as he readied to jump. He leaped in the air, extended his foot, but before he could shove it in my face, I dissolved into my cloud of smoke. He kicked the ground, landing with a grunt. I materialized behind him shoving my claws into his back drawing more blood.

Oleg collapsed on the ground, arching his back. He flew into the air, spun around and screamed as he charged me.

Even though Oleg was a large Viking, he hardly had any powers. He was strong and could glamor humans, but he had no power against vampires. He had even enquired at the Vampire Council why, and they couldn't answer him. But the moment he grabbed hold of you, he didn't let go. His powerful arms could crush a vampire and he would use that power to tear my head from my body. All I had to do was run circles around him until I found a gap.

Before Oleg slammed his body into mine, I burst into my smoke and floated above his head. As much fun as this was, it bored me. It had to end.

I landed a short distance away from him, pulled out the dagger from behind my back and charged. He collided with me with a painful thud, knocking my head backward. He wrapped his meaty arm around my neck while the other went around my chest. I maneuvered the dagger to my side and shoved it into his thigh. He shrieked, let go of me, and reached for the opened wound. He growled when he noticed it wasn't closing and he wasn't healing.

"What is that made of?"

"I warned you, Oleg. I'm done playing your stupid games. A warlock charmed my dagger against lesser vampires, and I'm glad to see it has enough juju to stop you."

My words only enraged him. He shouldered my

abdomen, knocking the dagger out of my hand. I elbowed his neck, which crunched, and his arms went limp. I jumped over his body and reached for the dagger once more. As I held it up, he ran into me. The hilt of the dagger stuck out of his diaphragm while the point lodged itself in his heart. Before I could utter my goodbye, he burst into flames and a gust of wind blew his ashes away.

"Good grief. That took longer than expected," I mumbled, cleaning the dagger on my pants as best I could. It probably needed another charm, which I'd do in a few days' time. But first, where was everybody?

Chapter Twenty-Nine

DECLAN

Lana stood before me like an angel. Her flowing white dress accentuating her curves, her hair cascading down her shoulders, and she stared lovingly at me with bright green eyes.

I cupped her warm face and bruised her lips. She moaned as her hands caressed my shoulders, then moved down to my waist and she wrapped her arms around me. She was warm and comfortable in the embrace. I never wanted to let her go. When I finally ended the kiss and stood back, her eyes were still closed, and her mouth parted.

"Is it always going to be like this?"

"Which part?" I kissed the tip of her nose.

"Everything." Her eyes flitted open and pinned me to my spot. "I've been here a month and you've done nothing but shower me with lovemaking, affection, and your undivided attention. Is this it, or are you going to change? Are you going to abandon me for other girls? I know you have vampire work to do but are you content with only me?" she asked carefully.

Her question caught me off guard, but not unexpectedly. I'd thought about what I wanted, whether I was satisfied with just having her. To test myself, I decided on smothering her with my affection every day to see whether I'd tire, and in this past month I hadn't. I hadn't once thought of another woman. Perhaps I was maturing—*heaven forbid*—or I'd finally found the right woman. My chest swelled with her warmth, and I knew it was her, I found the right one.

I caressed my lips against hers and combed my fingers through her hair; the fine strands of sandy-brown hair curling around my wrist.

"I admit I was never a one lady kind of man. But as it turns out, I just never met the right one. When we first met, I was unsure, you made me feel things I never wanted to admit to. But, after much dark soul searching, I'm happy to relay that I'm extremely happy with my purchase. I'd like to keep you, if you'll have me."

She slapped my chest as the corners of her mouth curved upward. "You're so silly," she said with a distinct nod. "Make me yours, baby."

In one swift motion, I picked up my prize and lowered her gently on the bed. "I'm going to feed on you, my love. Then I'm going to bind you to me. Much like I did with Ursula, except yours comes with an orgasm." I wiggled my eyebrows.

She grabbed my shirt and pulled me down so I could nip at her pale column. Her pulse throbbing beneath her skin, the smell of her blood driving me crazy. I ripped her dress to shreds and removed my clothing as fast as my vampire powers allowed.

Her warm body hummed in anticipation as I covered her in my kisses. In my excitement to bond with her, I didn't bother with any foreplay and dug right in. Her ripe body begged for release, and she whimpered as I sucked in a nipple while massaging the other. I settled myself between her legs and pushed the tip inside her heated sheath. Lana clutched my shoulders as I slowly eased inside, coating my shaft with her juices.

Every muscle in her body relaxed as I continued my pleasurable wrath on her body. I heard the rhythm of her heart and felt it beat against the breast I was sucking.

Each thrust tore a series of moans from her, and I captured her mouth with mine. Her lips were soft and firm, my tongue caressing hers in a series of languid strokes that sent sparks of pleasure through me and left her hungry for more.

Lana's eyes rolled into the back of her head as her desire bloomed through her, no longer able to respond to me. I smiled knowingly as I enclosed my vampire powers around her in a cocoon of love and protection. To complete the bonding, I needed to bite her delicate skin.

My hips jerked as I sought release, the thrilling sensation pushing us right to the edge. I held her firmly in place as I pumped, sinking my teeth into her. In that moment our orgasm smacked into us, a flood of toe-curling, sensual spasms knocked the breath out of her while I drank down her exotic blood. Her life essence swirled around me, and I offered her everything; what I had left of my soul, my dark heart, my mind and my body.

Lana moaned, accepting me as I was while my powers reached inside her, binding her to me for a lifetime. The darkness within me brightened as my pulse, or her pulse, raced through my veins and it felt like I was on fire.

My movements slowed, I unhooked my teeth and licked the wound. I mumbled the words needed for the bonding, making us one.

Lana stared at me with hooded eyes and a lazy smile.

"I love you," she mumbled before my numbing venom took hold of her.

"I love you, too." I kissed her chastely, pulled her into the curve of my body and listened to her sleep. I would lie with her until she came down from her vampire high, and we would start the rest of our lives together.

www.vinci-books.com/fixer

**They say demons burn... but maybe that's exactly what I
need.**

You only bargain with a demon when you're desperate. I was. But
the Fixer isn't the monster I expected—he's beautiful, dangerous,
and impossible to resist. Now he's here to collect, and my heart's
part of the price.

Turn the page for a free preview...

The Fixer: Chapter One

MADDOX

It took little to hear my name being called. Those in peril need only whisper '*Fixer*' and I'd hear them. Then I'd snap my fingers and follow the directions to their location.

"Fixer," she called again, more despondent. She's a young woman, alone, and desperately needed my help.

I exhaled and stood up.

"Wait, Fixer, you can't go yet," Jack groaned, blood and spittle looped across his teeth and down his broken jaw. "You didn't do what you said you would," Jack continued in that painful, monotonous tone.

"Jack, I've been lenient with you. It's time to collect." I rolled my shirt sleeves to my elbows. "If you can't hold your end of the bargain, then you know what's going to happen."

Jack whimpered, pushed himself onto his elbows and dragged his body toward the exit, leaving a bloody trail behind him.

"I didn't say you could go," I said sinisterly and closed the gap.

I reached for Jack's shoulder and belt, and in one swift

motion, I threw him across the floor. He skidded, slamming into the far wall with a loud groan and a fresh head wound.

"Please, Fixer, my family—"

"You should've thought of them before asking for my help," I said, stalking Jack.

He cried. The wounds from his forehead, cheek and arms seeping blood, pooling beneath him.

I rarely revealed my true features for fear of hurting, or worse, killing humans. Humans were such fragile creatures, so easily disturbed and pathetic. Few survived the mental break, while others resorted to killing themselves. Only to join my family and fellow demons in the Underworld.

"No, no, no...," Jack continued, his lips swollen. "Please—"

I couldn't wait for him to finish his pathetic sentence. I had enough. The world slowed down. My hands morphed into large, dark claws with sharp, metallic fingernails. My body grew double in size as I watched Jack's eyes slowly widen.

My face darkened into my demonic features—a face only a mother would love—and my horns extended out of my forehead. My black wings expanded behind me and I rolled my shoulders, stretching my neck.

The world picked up speed until the air swirled around us normally.

"No, Fixer, please."

The stench of urine wafted in the air, along with rotten eggs. I narrowed my eyes at his pants, which had darkened near the crotch area.

"Please..." he continued his plea.

"I gave you three chances, Jack. Three!" I shouted. "If anyone found out, they'd stop being afraid. I can't have that."

I lunged at him, gripped him by the shoulders, and yanked him off the floor. I dug my fingernails into his soft flesh until I struck the wall behind him. His screams were music to my ears. His blood fueled my hunger, and I lapped it up hungrily.

I sliced through his meat with my talons, cut through his chest bones, the sound echoing in the cavernous room, and reached for his beating heart.

Jack's eyes rolled back when I squeezed the organ in my hand. The natural pump struggled to beat in my grasp.

Jack's jaw slackened and his last breath escaped his chapped lips.

His dark soul screamed out of his body and I sucked that in. My eyes glowed brightly, like they did every time I fed on souls. The darker the better. My skin tingled and a low growl of satisfaction escaped my lips.

I dropped Jack's limp body, watching it crumple to the floor.

"Maddox!" someone yelled outside, followed by a door blown off its hinges.

That was my cue to escape and follow the moans of the distressed female.

The Fixer: Chapter Two

MADDOX

The distress call sounded from an apartment building in New York. The victim was a mother, holding her child.

"Fixer," she cried, with mascara running down her cheeks as she rocked the corpse in her arms. "Please help me."

I shook my head. The boy was dead; there was nothing I could do to bring him back. I could offer him comfort as he moved to the afterlife in the Underworld; ensure his safety, but that was it.

But to tell a grieving mother was like sticking a hot coal in her face. They wouldn't hear a word I said, only the breaking of their heart.

"He's gone, my dear," I whispered.

Her cries softened as she clutched onto his body, mumbling words I never wanted to mutter. Words begging for forgiveness. Words filled with heartache. Words filled with remorse.

I didn't have to punish her. She'd do so on her own and repeatedly until she joined her son.

I couldn't watch the depressing show any longer and glanced around her two-bedroom apartment, which was small yet cosy. The kitchen neat with a half-filled mug of coffee on the counter.

The living area was large enough for a couch, coffee table, and television. On the coffee table beside the mirror, laced with a white powder, sat a loaded gun, and empty bottles of beer.

A large, naked man from the waist up sat on the couch near the narcotics and weapon, scowling at me.

I arched an eyebrow, and he quickly averted his eyes.

When he glanced at the drugs, he wiped his dirty nose with an even dirtier finger and proceeded to snort a line, not caring I was there. But before he could bring the rolled up note to his nose, I smacked the mirror out of his hands and watched it shatter on the floor.

The man darted out of his seat. I pushed my metallic index nail into his neck, drawing blood. The man froze. His eyes wide as saucers, his blood dripping down his sweaty, hairy chest.

"Don't test me. I'm hungry," I said, sniffing near the man's bald head. "Although I'm not that hungry, your stench and rotting soul would only give me a stomach ache."

The man shook with fear the moment I yanked my fingernail out of his flesh, but he dared not move. His eyes remained on mine, his mouth parted in a surprised O and his blood oozed out of the fresh wound.

I stepped backward and blinked. His shoulders relaxed slightly, and he exhaled.

"Is that yours?" I pointed at the white powder.

The man nodded slowly without taking his eyes off me.

"I didn't know the boy was home—"

I raised my hand, silencing him. "I don't want to hear it. It's yours. The boy is dead. Therefore, it's your fault. Do you agree?"

His eyes flitted to the woman and child on the floor, then back to me.

"Is it your fault?" I yelled, making him flinch.

"Yes... yes, it's my fault," he cried, finally realizing his blood was running down his body, and pressed a dirty hand to the cut. "But—"

"No!" I closed the distance, grabbed him by the throat and squeezed.

The man gripped my arm, trying to pry me off him.

My vise grip needed more than just human strength to get me off him and squeezed tighter; like squishing a grape. I crushed his larynx and broke his spine.

The man seized to exist, his black soul seeped out of his pores like dark ink and I didn't consume it; my cousins in the Underworld could have their fill of him. I dared not taste this disgusting man.

The woman behind me sobbed louder upon seeing her husband's demise, let go of her dead son and crawled to his corpse.

"What did you do? Now they're both gone. How can I carry on?"

"You should've thought of that before calling me, dear," I growled, crouching near her quivering body. "Now about payment," I whispered as I looked her over. She was fit, a slender body, a little too much makeup, but I could smear it off her face with my thumb. "What can you offer me?" I grabbed her wrist and pulled her to her feet.

She whimpered from the sudden movement, but the moment I cupped her cheeks, she stilled. It was only us surrounded by my darkness. Her eyes glazed over as I stared at her, forcing her into submission.

I combed my fingers through her hair and her trembling body stilled. She relaxed in my embrace and I brought her closer to my body.

The same stench I smelled on the man I smelled on her, too. I wrinkled my nose and stepped back, letting her go.

She blinked, confusion stamped all over her face, but the moment she noted the man on the floor and her dead son, she wailed again.

I exhaled and shook my head. At this rate, I'd be staying hungry.

The Fixer: Chapter Three

KINSLEY

"Mom!" I yelled, closing the front door. "Rosie? Ben?" I called, crossing the entrance hall and into the kitchen. "Where is everyone?" I mumbled to myself as I opened the fridge door and stared at the contents, but instead of taking out the delicious pudding or the freshly made chicken casserole, nausea made its way into my mouth and I swallowed hard, shuddering at the aftertaste. "Ugh," I grumbled and closed the door.

When continued silence echoed around me, I entered the living area, and ice filled my veins. The grisly scene in front of me cleared my brain of thought and my body of moving.

My dad on the new Persian carpet with a pool of dark liquid beneath him. I couldn't be certain what the liquid was until flashes of the gaping wounds to his head, cheek, and chest filled my mind.

I clutched at my chest, ensuring my heart was still beating, and exhaled a shaky breath.

My mother sat beside my dad with her favorite chopping knife in her bloodied hands. Her bloody clothing shredded with scratch marks on her inner thighs and across her chest like a wild animal had attacked her.

"Mom?" I mouthed soundlessly. I cleared my throat, but it was too dry.

I crossed the threshold but stopped on the edge of the maroon liquid marking the white carpet. Dread washed over me at the repercussions of what lay ahead; flash photography; reporters; police; questions; abuse; rape; murder. At the center were my parents, and everyone would ask where I was when this took place. Why didn't I stop it? Why didn't I help?

I choked on a sob. "Mom," I whispered after finding my voice. "What happened?" I whimpered.

Mom continued rocking, staring at the knife, then at my father's gutted corpse.

"Mom," I said softly and reached for her shoulder. The moment I touched her, she glanced at me with recognition in her emerald colored eyes and her bottom lip trembled.

"He did it again, Kinsley," she said, placing the knife on the carpet, leaving her bloody fingerprints. She glanced at my father, then stood up. "He came at me again," she whimpered, her body shaking as the adrenaline wore off. "He came for me. I couldn't take it. Not again. I had to stop him this time. You know he wouldn't stop until one of us was dead—"

"I know," I shushed her. "I know," I repeated, reaching for her hand. "Let's get you cleaned up. Now where's Rose and Ben?"

"Uh," she said, glancing around. "Your dad gave them the day off. You know he does that when he wants to be alone with me."

The moment I touched her, she burst into uncontrollable tears. I pulled her into an embrace, never wanting to let go. I wanted to hold her until she felt no pain, until she felt safe, and could be herself again.

I couldn't allow my mother to be tormented by the police because she put down the actual monster. I couldn't allow her to be hurt by the rest of my family, embarrassed by the public, and humiliated by the police.

They would tear her down until there was nothing left of her. She would wither away, leaving me. I'd be all alone.

I held onto my mother, squeezing my eyes shut. When I opened them, I glanced around and became nauseated once more. I couldn't...

I needed someone to take care of this. Someone discreet, and could easily dispose of a body or make it look like an accident.

This needed to be fixed. I needed *The Fixer*.

"Fixer!" I said loud enough before I thought too long and hard about it. We couldn't wait for my dad's body to decompose while we thought of a way to dispose of him. The council would ask where he was. He was influential and always in the public eye and people would know he went missing if he didn't respond to messages on time.

I knew going into any deal with The Fixer could get me killed, or worse, destroy my family. But we needed him now. We needed him to take care of this. Whatever the consequences were, I'd deal with them. Just as long as I kept my mother safe.

I swallowed hard. Wind whipped my face, although the doors and windows were shut.

Mother cowered beside me. I wrapped my arm around her, pulling her closer, and covered my stomach.

A thick darkness spread from the light fixture and descended, materializing into a man with an ominous shadow. He lifted his head higher and glared down at me like I was dessert. His eyes flitted to mother, then to father's body. A sinister smile crept up his face. It was then I realized I made a mistake.

Grab your copy...
www.vinci-books.com/fixer

About the Author

A Multi-genre author writing twisted endings...

N Gray is a USA Today Bestselling Author who lives in Cape Town, South Africa, with her daughter and adopted cat named Miss Beans.

During the day, she's an analyst and provider profiler for a medical insurance company. At night, she types on her curved keyboard, creating fictional characters some may love and others you want to kill yourself.

She writes in four genres: urban fantasy, thriller, horror, and paranormal romance.

She now writes under Natalie Michaels for her new thrillers and SD Syns for her new horrors.

Acknowledgments

Thank you to my readers, old and new, for taking a chance on my books.

You are the reason I write the stories I do. As long as you keep reading, I'll keep writing.

I'm truly humbled by your support and encouragement.

I write in as many genres as I love reading in. There are so many stories swarming inside my head that I could never just choose one.

Horror is my guilty pleasure. I love writing short stories filled with dark humour and the occult, with a twist ending.

Urban fantasy and paranormal romance are where I love to spend my time, and I have so many books planned that I don't have enough time *(but I'll get there)*.

And lastly, my thrillers. Who doesn't love sitting on the edge of their seat while reading about what goes on inside the antagonist's mind? Well, I love writing about them.

www.ingramcontent.com/pod-product-compliance
Lightning Source LLC
Chambersburg PA
CBHW011749010726
47498CB00012B/2994